Myra,

Marathon Journey, An Achilles Story

By Stephen F. Balsamo

I hope that this story can show people the greatness of your dad — and show how much I respect him.

Afterword Written by Marathon Legend, Dick Traum

Stephen F. Balsamo

Wayne,

I hope that this story will show these people the greatness of your dad — and how much I respect him.

[illegible signature]

Dedicated to:

-Regina

-The Lost Boys of Sudan

-Dr. Romeo Zamora

-Dick Traum and Team Achilles

-Mrs. Tessie Minor

-my parents

Mile 1

Southern Sudan, early 1990's

The lion sat still in the high grass. The only movements from the majestic and powerful animal were his eyes, which scanned the surroundings. Atop a small rolling hill overlooking the flatlands, the lion was at a prime vantage point to take in the beauty of Southern Sudan. Various shades of remarkable colors filled the sky as a perfectly round crimson sun slowly descended, appearing as if it were melting into the earth far off on the horizon. But the lion was not there to take in the view. Sunset was prime hunting time and, although not moving, the lion was most certainly searching for prey.

Some rustling to the right alerted the lion to the presence of something. With a slight turn of its head, an object came into view. It was a nine-year-old boy. The lion dipped deeper into the grass and watched intently as the boy walked slowly.

A native of Southern Sudan, the boy knew the land well; he should have known that a lion could be lurking in the weeds. Oblivious to the danger, the boy, who was about twenty feet away, was walking a path that would put him directly in front of the lion in a matter of seconds.

Shielded by the high grass, the lion waited patiently as it allowed the boy to walk closer so that the attack would be easier. The lion tensed its body as the boy, who was ever so close to the attack zone, took some more steps. After the boy took another step, the wait was over. The lion's muscles contracted and catapulted into action. The big cat sprung up in a fluid motion fueled by remarkable power and accompanied with a terrifying roar.

The boy looked to his left and saw what was coming.

He turned and ran with all the might and energy he could muster, but the fear running through his body seemed to sap him of speed. While running as fast as he could, he felt as if he had a heavy weight on his back. Without even turning, he could tell the lion was rapidly gaining ground because the roars, which emanated from inside the beast and crossed over its powerful jaws, were getting louder with each passing second.

Running and screaming, the boy headed towards a great big tree about ten yards ahead with the hope that he could find safety and refuge in its high branches which he had climbed on with his friends on countless occasions.

The thunderous sound of paws rapidly striking the earth signaled to the boy that escape was impossible. His running slowed to feeble and clumsy steps before the lion took him down to the ground feet from the tree.

The boy twisted and rolled over onto his back in an effort to defend himself.

He said, "Adamu, you are too fast for me. And your nails are too long. No scratching. No scratching. And no biting."

Adamu, also a nine-year-old boy, was taking the role of the lion in the game seriously. He was grinning broadly, which prominently displayed his teeth, and his fingers and thumbs were bent in to give the impression that he had claws. As his roars turned to laughter, he thrust his hands down and playfully clawed at Naeem's chest and stomach.

At that moment, two more nine-year-old boys ran by, and Adamu jumped up with a roar and chased after them.

Along with the lion persona, he ran after his friends with a magnificent and exuberant free spirit attainable only in the precious time of life known as childhood.

Narrowly escaping capture, Dukarai and Salim had reached the tree, which was the pre-determined safety zone where lion attacks were prohibited. Adamu quickly reverted back to a nine-year-old, and ran over to help Naeem up from the ground.

The strong bond between the four children transcended mere friendship. They were all born the same year and, since infancy, they had spent their days together in a village of clustered huts in Southern Sudan. Each of their families, like all families in the village, were very close. It was acceptable and understood that it was the responsibility of the elders from all families to help raise the children in the village. Adamu, Naeem, Salim, and Dukarai were as close to brothers as children who were not related could ever be.

The four laughed together as they congregated under the tree. One game was finished, but there were endless things the boys could find to do. There was always something new to experience.

Pointing to the quarter of the sun that was still visible on the horizon, Salim, with a hint of disappointment, said, "Look, the sun is almost gone for the day."

While the number of adventures that the boys could find to do together was endless, they were required to complete their fun by the time the sun went down.

"Well, then we should chase it," Adamu declared.

"Chase what?" Dukarai inquired.

"The sun. We should chase after it," Adamu answered. "If we get close to it we can get more time to play and explore. While the sun is setting here, it is still up somewhere else."

"Yeah, we should do that," Dukarai said excitedly.

"Yeah, we can keep running and running all around the world and get a full day of sunlight," Naeem added as he agreed with the far-fetched idea.

Salim jumped up and down and said, "We could explore the whole world!"

They laughed at the beautiful fantasy of the plan that they all knew was impossible.

With confidence and conviction, Adamu shouted, "Okay, let's go. Let's chase the sun," as he led the group on a high-speed sprint directly towards the beautiful setting sun far off on the horizon.

Years later, as the boys grew closer to adulthood, games and explorations gave way to duties and responsibilities. In about a year when Adamu, Naeem, Dukarai, and Salim reached age twenty, they would join the men herding cattle. In the rainy season of April through September, they would work to herd the cattle to higher ground and, when the waters subsided, drive the cattle back to the flatlands. Until that time, and in preparation of the impending responsibilities of adulthood, the four friends were charged with the duty of clearing the fields so the millet crops could be planted.

Struggling to break up the dry ground, Salim stopped working for a moment and looked far off in the distance at Lafon Hill.

Clearly visible about ten miles away, the very large Lafon Hill, standing by itself on the flatlands, stood out without equal.

"We never got to the top of Lafon Hill like we said we would," Salim observed.

"We just started and Salim is already daydreaming," Dukarai said to the others.

"No, really. We always said we would get to the top one day, but we never did," Salim reminded his friends.

Lafon Hill was indeed a long time lure to the four adventurous boys who had explored nearly every inch of their immediate surroundings. With resignation, Salim added, "Soon enough we will be too busy herding cattle to do anything," as he vigorously resumed his digging. It was early morning and a long day of work was ahead. The conversation ceased for an hour or so as they spread out to different areas and focused on the task at hand.

Adamu, Dukarai, and Naeem's concentrated efforts were broken when they heard Salim yelling out as he ran from the direction of the village back towards the field.

Without the others noticing, Salim had slipped away from the field.

With a big smile on his face, and through giddy laughter, he announced, "Stop. No work today!"

Adamu, Naeem, and Dukarai looked at each other with incredulous looks of surprise. Salim had somehow convinced the elders that they could have a reprieve from work for the day. They did not even ask how Salim had convinced the elders to excuse them from their duties, for it did not matter.

Just as they did when they were little kids, they quickly banded together and shared a hearty round of laughter. They had another precious day to relive their childhood.

"Okay, what are we to do?" Adamu asked.

Pointing far off in the distance Salim answered, "Lafon Hill. Today we make it to the top."

While Salim was able to get them out of having to do their chores, his idea of what to do was not exactly a leisurely way to spend the day. It would take a good effort to reach the top of Lafon Hill and return.

"What? Lafon Hill? Come on Salim. That is a long haul," Naeem voiced what both Adamu and Dukarai were also thinking.

"That is the only way out of the field work. It is either that or work. And you know what? We will always be able to say that we did it together."

All four agreed. Today would be the day they would meet their long elusive goal of conquering Lafon Hill.

"I cannot wait to be at the top while I wait for all of you to catch up," Salim said as he set down the challenge to the others.

"Oh, we will see about that," Dukarai responded.

"Well, let's get going. We don't have all day," Adamu said.

"Oh, yes, we do," Salim said as they left their work behind and headed towards Lafon Hill. For the first hour, the four slowly roamed and meandered as they happily got distracted by various discoveries and observations.

When Lafon Hill appeared closer, their path straightened out and their pace increased to a rapid walk, then to a jog, and then to an all-out run. The friendly competition of who among them would reach the top of Lafon Hill first was officially underway. Side by side all four friends ran together on a clear beautiful Sudanese day. In reality, all four knew that it would not really be a competition.

Naeem, Salim, and Dukarai knew that they would be battling for second place. They had recognized long ago that Adamu possessed the gift of speed.

Adamu, knowing that he had the ability to separate from his friends at any time, ran side by side with them for miles so that he could enjoy the glorious day with them. But when they were about a mile from the base of the hill, Adamu increased his pace. The others tried in vain to match his acceleration, but they quickly abandoned their efforts.

Despite securing a tremendous lead, Adamu kept increasing his speed.

He loved the feel of his bare feet gripping the earth, the sight of the countryside as he propelled across it, and the joy in his soul from running.

From far behind, Adamu heard Salim yell out words of encouragement, "Go, Adamu, go!"

Filled with adrenaline and excitement from knowing he was on the precipice of accomplishing something he and his friends had talked about for years, Adamu ran even faster when he started up the hill despite the progressive incline. When he made it to the top he raised his arms, not in victory, but in celebration of an accomplishment on a beautiful day in the land he loved.

The stunning elevated view was even better when his friends joined him. They hugged and congratulated each other as they all took in the view.

It did not matter what order they made it to the top; they had accomplished their goal together.

Mile 2
Oregon, early 1970's

The cool Oregon air breezed through the campus and descended upon the members of the track team as they were preparing for practice. When Coach Paul Bellinger blew his whistle three times to alert the team that practice was about to start, William Caldwell tied up his laces, peeled off his hooded pull-over, and ran to join his teammates around the coach.

Bradford, a small picturesque college, was primarily known for its solid academics, not its sport programs, but the track team was earning a reputation as a winning outfit.

Despite decades of being a perennial low finisher in the standings, the team had been steadily improving since Coach Bellinger took over the program. Now it was a strong contender for the conference championship.

As the brisk wind blew some leaves across the track, the coach implored, "Okay, guys, let's go, pick it up, pick it up."

A young coach in his early thirties, Coach Bellinger, a former college track standout, looked fit enough to be a member of the team. Recently married, he had just bought a home where he and his wife intended to raise a big family. Before his wedding day he looked to the future with some fear and trepidation, but he now found himself enthusiastically embracing all of the ever-increasing responsibilities and challenges in his life.

Besides helping to elevate their running ability, Coach Bellinger cultivated an environment of selflessness among the team; it was a true team in every sense of the word. William and the other seniors, who were part of the coach's first recruiting class, were loyal to him. They desperately wanted to win Bellinger his first championship as a coach.

An average student in high school, William did not seriously consider college until his senior year when his high school coach told him that the new coach at Bradford was going to scout him at the next meet.

The interest from Bradford was the impetus for William to run with maximum effort at the meet where won the 1500 meter race. William met with Coach Bellinger after the meet and was quickly impressed with his enthusiasm.

During one of William's recruiting trips to Bradford, Coach Bellinger arranged a lunch with a number of other recruits. The energetic coach told each recruit he believed they could play a role in turning the lowly Bradford track team into a championship contender while earning a degree and having a lot fun along the way. At the end of the lunch, Coach Bellinger stood up, dimmed the lights, plugged in a slide projector, and showed slides of each recruit from various meets. While showing the pictures, he recited a glowing summary of their respective accomplishments.

Everyone laughed when Coach Bellinger showed a picture of a very muddy William, looking dejected after a rainy cross country meet, and said, "Here is a picture of William wishing he chose basketball."

The presentation made each recruit feel special and further illustrated the coach's commitment to the track program. Coach Bellinger made joining a losing team seem attractive, because it was clear that, under his guidance, the team would quickly turn into a winner.

In addition to excelling at track, William also flourished in the classroom at Bradford. He attributed much of his academic success to Coach Bellinger who preached that accomplishment could only be achieved through dedicated hard work.

Besides good grades, William's renewed academic spirit had other positive results. While studying in the library he met the love of his life, Christina. A serious student, Christina encouraged him to give his best effort in the classroom. Despite the demands of running track, studying, and being in a serious relationship, William was on his way to graduate with honors.

As his team surrounded him in a semi-circle, Coach Bellinger thrust his right arm into the middle of the group and said, "Okay, everybody in here, let's go."

Everyone on the team extended an arm and placed their hands on top of each other's and weakly said "Bradford" in unison.

Not happy with the level of the team's enthusiasm, Coach Bellinger kept his hand where it was as the members of his team were already stepping away.

The coach quickly directed, "Guys, back in here. Again, we are not done with this season. Nothing is guaranteed. We need to finish strong and focus on every single step along the way. Okay? So, come on, let's go, let's do what we have to do. Leave everything you have out on that track the rest of the way. There are just two weeks until the conference meet. We have to keep the focus and intensity. The success we are having should not be a reason for us to take it easy. You will have plenty of time to rest after the season. I want all of you to feel how great it is be part of a conference championship team. I have felt it and I want you to have it. It is something that will stay with you for your entire life. Let's have a strong practice."

In unison, everyone enthusiastically shouted, "Bradford."

Satisfied, Coach Bellinger implored, "Okay, good, let's get it going." As he stepped away from the center of the circle, Coach Bellinger patted William on the backside and said, "Keep it up, William, looking good, looking good, let's finish strong."

After warming up, the team began a series of 200 meter runs. Coach Bellinger, a strong proponent of speed work, made the series of 200 meter runs a central part of the team's practice. On numerous occasions, William would almost gleefully describe the horrifically brutal first practice in his freshman year when the coach had the team run one 200 meter after another. Each time William retold the story, the number of runs that he said Coach Bellinger made them do seemed to increase by two, but he always ended the tale with the same line which was entirely true: "Then Coach Bellinger came up to us after the last one and said *'OK, good, now let's start practice.'* "

Without a doubt, for William, running was a commitment to suffering, and he embraced it. Running long, running hard. Running early in the morning, late in the night, in the heat, in the cold, none of it mattered; he had to get his running in.

Pushing his body to the limit and then pushing it again to try to reach another limit. He found a perverse comfort in the light-headedness, the scorching burning of lactic acid in his legs, and the unsettling feeling in his gut when he was running further and faster and in conditions that a human body could not comfortably endure.

When he was in the zone, he relished it, for he knew that he could only achieve his goals if he reached that rarefied state of athletic physical trauma and had the mental fortitude to tolerate it.

In his final year, William was putting it all together. He was regularly winning and placing high at meets and he felt like he was getting better and stronger each week. Besides the typical aches and pains that any athlete was bound to be burdened with, William was running as injury free as he could hope. Everything was clicking and operating perfectly like a highly tuned sports car. He was peaking at the right time in the season, and he was confident that, at the conference championship, he would win the 1500 meters, and the team would win the overall title.

As he approached a turn on the track in one of the 200 meter runs, his breathing and pace were perfect when he noticed that some leaves and acorns had blown onto the track. In an effort to avoid stepping on the debris, William attempted to simultaneously extend his stride and move to his left.

His left foot landed awkwardly and he could not avoid stepping on an acorn. He felt his left knee pop. In the milliseconds before his body skidded on the track to a stop, and before any doctor told him what the MRI revealed, William already knew he had torn the ACL, the anterior cruciate ligament, in his knee. He had heard enough about what it was like to tear an ACL to know that his just tore apart. The scrapes and bruises on his hands and forehead would be the least of his concerns.

The torn ACL ended his running career, depriving him of his last opportunity to win the 1500 meter title and to be part of a championship team.

Sitting behind a desk littered with papers, files, and books, the man continued reading despite the ringing phone. On the fourth ring he took himself away from the written word, picked up the phone, and answered the call by saying his full name into the receiver.

Just as a floor littered with sawdust came with the territory in a carpenter's shop, a seemingly messy and unorganized office was part of being a lawyer. Despite the cluttered state, William Caldwell knew what was on his desk and in which pile it could be found.

After he graduated from Bradford College, William went to law school, married his girlfriend Christina, and raised two kids in a cozy community close to Bradford.

While he was grateful for his career, which qualified as a success, he realized that his job had its rewards, but was not necessarily rewarding. Late nights and weekends were often spent at the office instead of with the family. The stress from the workday followed him home and intruded into his family time too frequently over the years.

Now with his children grown, he recognized he could not get back the precious time lost, and that understanding helped to breed frustration.

Years earlier he and Christina would talk about how great it would be to have a quiet house all to themselves when their two kids were off to college. But he learned that there was a significant difference between a quiet house and a silent house after his eldest child, Jessica, married and moved to Seattle and when his son, Nicholas, decided to go to college across the country at New York University.

They both missed the kids and could not remember why they ever thought it would be enjoyable to have the house to themselves.

Not that he looked forward to working long hours in a demanding job for years to come, but William had started to think that retirement, something that he used to look forward to, might not be as great as he expected.

Christina had urged him to consider changing careers over the years, but he could not figure out what else to do. Also, the mortgage and other expenses, especially the high cost of putting his kids through college, had to be paid. He felt he was stuck, and he had no choice but to trudge along.

To make matters worse, the sedentary nature and time demands of his job led him to follow an unhealthy lifestyle. His expanding mid-section distorted his once athletic body and the mounting stress and frustration had defeated the free spirit he had in college.

Although his law office was near his old college, William was a long way in body and spirit from Bradford.

Mile 3

Exhausted from the long journey to the top of Lafon Hill and back, Adamu was in a deep sleep. Then a noise, that he first thought was a passing storm, woke him in the middle of the night. When he realized he was hearing gunfire and screams, he knew something was terribly wrong.

"Wake up! Get up!" Adamu's father, Nabil, shouted. "We must go now. We are being attacked. We must go!" The family scurried to their feet and followed Nabil out of the hut.

A young man, just about the same age as Adamu, aggressively ran at them with a torch extended high in the air.

Protecting his family, Nabil met his advance and grabbed the man's wrist and bent it back. The torch fell, and Nabil struck the attacker in the face with a punch that knocked him to the ground.

But just as quickly as Nabil defended his family from one attacker, two more appeared. One was armed with a club, the other with a machine gun.

Without words, the gunman fired.

The force of the bullets that riddled Nabil's body pushed him back several feet and seemed to keep him upright for a moment. When the firing stopped, the loving father and husband fell to the ground. Blood poured from his body, and his face was unrecognizable.

"Don't move. Stay still," the attackers ordered when Adamu's older brother Garai screamed out and ran towards his father. When Garai continued, shots rang out again and he dropped to the ground.

Adamu was paralyzed with fear and shock at the incomprehensible incident that seemed to happen so fast and so slow at the same time. Adamu wrapped his arms around his mother and sister, who clung onto him tightly.

"Let's go, let's go, this way," they ordered as they sought to separate the three remaining members of the loving family.

Two powerful club strikes just below Adamu's left knee, followed by one to his head, dropped Adamu to the ground as he lost hold of his mother and sister, who were quickly marched away.

Adamu tried to follow, but yet another club strike knocked him down. Face down in the dirt, the blood flowing from the bodies of his father and brother seeped onto his face and lips.

When he felt an intense heat, Adamu knew his hut, the center of his simple, happy, tranquil, and beautiful life, the place where he lived and shared the love of his family, was on fire.

When Adamu tried to climb to his feet, the torch was turned onto him—instantly penetrating his skin. As he twisted his body in pain, the attacker continued to force the torch down and dragged it across Adamu's back, over his right deltoid, and down his arm, leaving a path of melted and blistered skin. When Adamu was able to turn over onto his back, the attacker repeatedly stabbed the torch down onto him as his body violently coiled and re-coiled from the pain.

The gunshots, the screams, and the light and heat of the crackling fire began to fade from Adamu's senses. In the midst of the chaos and destruction, the violent movements in his body reacting to the burns slowed to a halt.

The cold water jolted him back from the darkness.

Tahir, Adamu's brother's best friend, was fleeing the village when he passed Adamu's burning hut. The sight of his good friend and Nabil lying dead in a pool of their blood brought him to a stop, and the slight movements from Adamu's practically lifeless body were enough for him to determine that Adamu could be saved.

He lifted Adamu off the ground, slung him over his broad shoulders, and ran out of the village and into a nearby river in an effort to stop Adamu's flesh from burning. After totally submerging Adamu in the water for a few seconds, Tahir held Adamu's head up so that he could breathe.

"What is this about?" Adamu wearily questioned as Tahir dug into the earth of the riverbank for mud to place over Adamu's burns in an attempt to ease his pain.

"It is the *djellabas* from the North. They are trying to take over Southern Sudan. They are killing all of our men."

Adamu could not begin to understand. They were Dinkas from a tiny village that raised cattle; they had nothing to do with politics and were not involved in any conflicts with anyone from the North.

"What about your family?" Adamu asked.

Tahir just shook his head and said, "No."

"Did you see my mother and sister?"

"No. They are taking all of the women. I don't know what happened to them. I did not see them."

"Tahir, what about Salim, Naeem, and Dukarai?" Adamu asked, his voice trembling with fear.

Tahir turned his head away. Looking at the burning village in the distance he said, "They have been slaughtered, Adamu. I am sorry."

Adamu was dealing with the greatest and most horrific physical and mental pain he ever experienced in the same river he had walked alongside on so many peaceful occasions listening to the wisdom of his father.

While seriously injured his life was not in jeopardy, but the blood flowing through his heart and the oxygen circulating in his lungs were just functions that merely allowed him to meet the medical definition of what constituted life. Without the village and the people who he loved, like a lake evaporated by drought, the essence of who Adamu was had vanished.

Tahir lifted Adamu out of the water and onto his shoulders.

"Adamu, you are all I have now. We must survive. We will survive. Both of us. I will get us to safety."

That night and the days and weeks over the nearly three months that followed, Tahir provided Adamu with the support that allowed him to endure. Swollen and discolored from the club strikes, Adamu's left leg was tender to the touch, and his debilitating burns did not stop delivering pain. The fatigue, hunger, thirst, injury, and profound sadness were all working in conjunction to overcome Adamu's will to live. But time and time again, Tahir was there to carry Adamu both physically and mentally.

Whenever Adamu told Tahir to leave him and continue without him, Tahir refused and encouraged Adamu to push on. He told Adamu that they were meant to live for some reason, and they were obligated to persevere.

Days into their flight, Tahir and Adamu met ten young men from Southern Sudan who were also forced from their village after it was attacked. Later the group met another five. Then, fifteen or so more joined. The expanding group was made up mostly of young men like Adamu and Tahir. They heard there was a refugee camp in Kenya. It was a long journey, but they would try to make it together.

They went days without anything to drink or eat. If they were lucky to come across *apai* grass, they chewed it to take in nutrients. If they found a dried-out riverbank, they dug into the wet mud and tried to suck the water from it. Some drank their own urine. The mosquitoes infected some with malaria, and the dirty water gave many diarrhea, but they continued walking.

Starvation, dehydration, disease, and attacks by militants and wild animals would claim the lives of many along the way, but they carried on. Through the darkness of night and the intense sun during the day, they kept moving forward. They walked hundreds of miles on dirt paths, through the forest, over swamplands, and across the desert, away from the country where they had lived their entire lives.

By the time they reached the refugee camp in the desert in Kenya, the group numbered close to one hundred.

They, and scores of other courageous young men, would be known to the world as the Lost Boys of Sudan.

After struggling to open his heavy eyelids, Adamu expended his limited energy to focus on the man who was hovering over him.

After he finished taking a close look at the bandages on Adamu's left shoulder, the man stepped back a few feet and wrote some notes on a clipboard.

"Hello, I am Dr. Zamora, your doctor at the Kakuma refugee camp hospital. You have been sleeping for a while now. The anesthesia we used for the surgery and the pain medication will keep you feeling drowsy. You had a pretty bad break on your left leg, but the infection from the burns was our biggest concern. It is amazing that you were able to make it all those miles in your condition. You are a survivor."

The words were not registering with Adamu, whose eyes wearily focused on the decorative flag pin with blue, white, and yellow colors attached to the lapel of the doctor's white shirt.

The exemplary treatment that Adamu received was truly extraordinary, yet typical of the work that the conscientious doctor from the Philippines provided to many others at the refugee camp.

At the moment, Adamu had no recollection whatsoever of even arriving at the camp, let alone being examined or being brought to an operating room.

The exhausting efforts to test his memory resulted in snapshot recollections: walking in the desert with the others, being propped up on the back of a flat bed truck, the speed of the truck, the wind whipping sand into his face, Tahir holding him on the bumpy ride and telling him they made it.

When his eyes finally lost connection with the doctor's pin, he saw the first Asian face he had ever seen in person.

He thought about the pain he had been feeling nearly every second throughout the long trek and waited to feel it somewhere in his body, but he could not feel it anywhere. The multiple medications were doing their job for the moment. He tried to prop himself up to speak, but the attempt did little except to override the medication as a stinging pain suddenly shot throughout his body.

"Don't try to move. Just relax," the doctor instructed. "You will be in bed for a while. You can start moving about when you get stronger. But that will have to wait."

Adamu tried to speak, but his tongue could not respond. The doctor benevolently placed a hand on his forearm and said, "I will check on you again soon," and swiftly moved on to tend to another patient.

Alone, Adamu scanned the dismal and cramped environment inside the medical tent that would house him for weeks. Dr. Zamora and his staff were far outnumbered by the numerous cots filled with Sudanese refugees suffering from a wide variety of maladies.

After he completed the visual tour of his dreary surroundings, all of the terrible things he had witnessed and experienced flashed through his mind, and a dreadful pain swelled from deep in his soul.

He closed his eyes, hoping for a sleep that might take his mind far away from his thoughts and memories.

Mile 4

Sunday morning, when he could wake up late, avoid shaving, and read the newspapers with Christina over coffee and bagels, was William's favorite part of the week.

Standing up to refill his mug, he asked, "So what happened to all of the things we said we would do when we finally had the house to ourselves?" After a sip of coffee, he filled the silence again by commenting, "We are getting old."

"Speak for yourself," Christina responded from behind the newspaper held in front of her face.

Unlike him, she was completely comfortable with her life and enjoyed it. As a fourth grade school teacher who loved her work, Christina was rejuvenated each year by teaching a new group of students. She had more interests, more friends, and more things to do than her husband.

After a moment she held her newspaper to the side so she could see him and said, "But it does seem that it is not as much fun having the house to ourselves as we thought it would be, right? If you want I can book a trip within an hour. You know how I always wanted to go to Paris."

William regretted saying anything.

While he enjoyed vacations with Christina, he was tired of the things that went hand in hand with a trip: the inevitable delays, sitting on a plane for hours, and sleeping in an uncomfortable bed.

She always felt a trip was the answer for pretty much anything, but he was not necessarily looking for somewhere to go.

He was looking for something to take him off autopilot for a while, to fill the void left with the kids leaving—something to re-energize his soul.

"I don't want to do something specifically or go somewhere. I don't know what I want. It's just with the kids gone and my job being the same day after day, it seems I'm missing something. I am tired and worn out. I know the kids are doing great, and I am happy about that, but they need my guidance and advice less and less. I miss them being around."

Recognizing that he was taking the conversation to a serious level, Christina flattened her newspaper on the table and looked at him.

"I know it is an adjustment. You know it was not the easiest thing for me when Jessica got married and moved to Seattle or when Nicholas chose to go to college in New York. But you have to try to find something to fill that void. Is there something you want to do?"

Exasperated, William responded, "I don't know. I don't know. If I did, I would do it."

"What would make you happy? What have you wanted to do for a long time, but haven't gotten the chance to do? Think outside the box. You might discover something you will really like."

"I don't know. Maybe it is just a phase. I am in some sort of a malaise."

"Sometimes you have to try to do something you might not necessarily think you would like. What about taking an Italian class? What if we take a dancing class together?" she asked in quick succession, in an effort to spark a brainstorming session.

"Yeah, right. I am done with studying, and I have no rhythm," he answered.

"What about exercise? And I don't mean golf." Christina was full of ideas now.

"I am old and fat," William said in his defense.

"Yeah, right. You are real old, William. Give me a break."

"You didn't say that I wasn't fat though. That is undeniable," he said smiling as he held his flabby mid-section with both hands and shook it up and down.

"Well, you can change that if you want. You *were* an athlete in high school and college in case you forgot," Christina reminded him.

He thought for a second and then said, "Boy, that seems like another lifetime."

"No, William, that was in this lifetime."

He took a look at the sports section and saw an article about someone from Oregon planning to run the New York City Marathon that day.

Holding up the newspaper so Christina could see the article, he jokingly proclaimed, "Next year!"

"Nothing's stopping you." Then she added with a smile, "We can make a trip out of it."

He looked at her, smirked dismissively, and flipped the sports section to the other side of the table.

He took a gulp of coffee, then a bite from a bagel, and picked up the front page of the first section of the newspaper.

He started reading an article with the headline: *"Thousands of Refugees Flee War-Torn Sudan."*

Mile 5

Saddled with pain and fatigue, covered with bandages, and connected to IV tubes, Adamu was confined to his cot in the medical tent for weeks. Far across the tent he could see the youngest patient. Instead of being in the presence of the warmth of the love of his family, or playing with friends, the small boy was restricted to a cot in the musty, hot medical tent receiving treatment.

The empty expression that the boy wore each and every day told Adamu that he also experienced and saw things that no one, especially an innocent child, should be exposed to.

When he was strong enough to get up and walk, the first thing Adamu did was to shuffle across the busy tent to talk to the boy.

"Young boy, my name is Adamu. How are you doing?"

The nine-year-old boy looked up with sad eyes and said, "Bad. I hurt a lot. I have no one. My parents are gone. I have nothing."

Adamu reached down and took the boy's hand, "What is your name?"

"Kirabo."

"Kirabo, I have had loss too. I will be your friend, okay?"

"Okay."

"I will look out for you, okay?"

"Okay."

"Will you look after me too?"

"Okay."

Months earlier, with his older brothers and father far from the village tending to the cattle herd, Kirabo stood just outside his hut with the round thatched roof on a hot cloudless day, lost in the midst of the uncomplicated thoughts of a child. Looking for his mother, he spotted her about thirty feet away, carrying a pot filled with water.

He used to watch her meticulously make the pots by hand.

She would mold the clay with vigor to the desired form, smooth the edges with care, artfully etch a design, apply color, and then place them in a hole in the ground covered with burning straw.

They were beautiful, just like her.

He remembered she was smiling at him when he looked at her walking that day, carrying the pot in what would be the last seconds of his innocence. He could not remember if he smiled back, but he prayed he did. Kirabo loved her more than anything else the universe had to offer, nothing could compare.

He did not want to remember anything else from that day, but the terrible images still dominated his thoughts; he could not turn them off.

Hearing a rumbling sound, Kirabo turned from looking at his mother's glance and saw a large group of strange men wearing outfits running through the village. The quiet tranquility of the day was shattered by the noises from the guns that they fired as they swarmed in all directions.

Looking back to his mother, Kirabo saw the pot explode and bits of clay and water burst into the air as his mother's body spun around and fell to the ground. Kirabo never saw her face again after she smiled at him just before the men arrived. In the future, when he had the ability to consider if there was something to be thankful for, he would be thankful that, the last time he saw her face, the smile she wore was for him.

Just then Dr. Zamora stopped by Kirabo's cot to check up on him.

"Adamu, I am glad to see you up. How is the leg? How are the burns?"

"Better. I am feeling better, doctor."

"Good. Now, Kirabo, how are you today?"

"Okay," Kirabo responded meekly.

Squatting down to Kirabo's cot, Dr. Zamora said, "Okay. Let me take a look at the leg," as he pulled back the bed sheet that was covering his young patient from the waist down.

With the sheet removed, Adamu learned for the first time that Kirabo's left leg was amputated just below the knee. Adamu's body went weak as the terrible feeling of pain and loss he was all too familiar with swelled in his stomach and permeated throughout his entire body. It wasn't fair. There was too much pain everywhere; it knew no boundaries.

As Dr. Zamora continued his examination, Adamu staggered outside. Feeling helpless and full of despair, he crumbled to the ground.

He was so numb that he could not even cry.

When he had arrived at the camp, Kirabo was near death. He was malnourished, dehydrated, and ill from drinking dirty water. He also had a severe infection from a deep cut on his left foot, which was spreading. Kirabo was immediately ushered into the examining room where Dr. Zamora determined that his left leg had to be amputated in order to save his life.

On his way out of the tent after he finished examining Kirabo, Dr. Zamora saw Adamu sitting on the ground.

"What is it Adamu?"

Looking down to the ground Adamu said, "He is just a boy Dr. Zamora. It is not right. He is just a boy...He did not deserve this...He is just a boy...I cannot take this anymore."

The doctor knelt down and took hold of Adamu by the shoulders. "You are right, Adamu. He does not deserve this. No one does. But the question is where do we go from here? We have to move forward." Dr. Zamora held him a little tighter and gave him a small shake, "Be strong, Adamu. Be there for Kirabo. Be strong for him and for yourself."

Adamu stood up and took a deep breath.

Consciously trying to summon strength from somewhere in his depleted spirit, he walked back into the medical tent. Struggling to maintain his composure, he was filled with sadness and sympathy as he looked at the little boy who, along with so many other losses, was deprived of the innocence of childhood.

The boy would have fit in well with him and his friends during the games they played and the explorations they carried out years earlier.

He knelt down beside the cot and held Kirabo's hand. "Remember, we are friends now. I will be here for you."

In a sign showing that he agreed and understood, the small boy nodded his head before his eyes closed for a deep sleep.

It was the first interaction Kirabo had with someone in a long time that had nothing to do with suffering, loss, or medical treatment.

Mile 6

Holding onto the chain link fence at the main gate of the camp with one hand, Adamu shielded his eyes from the sun and the sand with his other hand so he could see all of the faces. The drained, gaunt, and lifeless faces of the new arrivals were not a sight Adamu liked to take in, but he had to look. Each and every time refugees made it to the camp he had to be there.

However, over the dozens of times he had faithfully carried out the inspections over the past six months, the faces of his mother and sister, which he ached to see, never materialized.

After he looked at the last of the unrecognizable faces of the group of twelve new refugees, he turned Kirabo's wheelchair to the direction of the playing field and pushed it in silence. Stopping under the shade of a tree, the two watched other refugees playing a competitive soccer game, but both were thinking of the faces that they again did not see despite the hope and prayers in their hearts.

"Are you going to play today?" Kirabo asked.

"Not today. My leg kind of hurts," Adamu responded, even though his leg did not hurt at all.

In fact, Adamu had made a great recovery. His leg, which Dr. Zamora conducted surgery on, had not hurt in months, and besides the permanent cosmetic damage, his burns had healed. He felt strong physically and had been playing soccer with the other refugees on a regular basis. He also found peace from running lap after lap around the grounds of the camp with Tahir each morning. In the midst of the painful and terrible thoughts that found a permanent place in his mind, running provided him with a bit of therapy.

He found a small level of comfort from the fact that he still was a fast runner.

Under normal circumstances Adamu would have played soccer, but he felt it was more important to stay close to Kirabo for the day, for he knew that his young friend was hurting because he too did not recognize any faces among the new arrivals.

"Did you play a lot of games in your village, Adamu?"

"Yeah, my friends and I would play all kinds of games. My favorite was when one of us would pretend to be a lion and then hunt each other down."

Adamu turned his fingers in on each hand to look like claws and, with a roar, playfully clawed at and tickled Kirabo's stomach.

The good-natured attack, which sought to make Kirabo laugh, failed to achieve its purpose. The boy did not even crack a slight smile.

Adamu realized Kirabo's life was devoid of laughter and smiles. There was nothing that Adamu, who was also hurting, could do to make the small boy laugh or to replace the sad expression he wore with a smile.

"What else did you and your friends play, Adamu?"

"When we got a little older my three friends and I would explore the land, and we would also race each other."

"Where would you go?"

Adamu thought for a moment and then recalled a very special memory.

"One day we went on a great exploration. Far from my village there is a big hill that sits on the flat lands all by itself far off on the horizon called Lafon Hill. For years my friends and I talked about how we wanted to make it to the top. Although it was a great distance, one day we decided to try to run to the hill. We were running side by side on the long run but, when we got closer, we all wanted to be the first one to make it to the top. So, about 100 yards away from the base of the hill, we started running as fast as we could. It was a fierce competition. Each of us took the lead at one time or another. And you know what?"

Kirabo, fully engrossed in the story, impatiently asked, "What? What?"

Knowing that he had a captive audience, Adamu paused for dramatic effect, and slowly continued his heavily embellished story.

"When we made it to the base of Lafon Hill, it looked more like a mountain, a giant mountain. It should be called Lafon Mountain. I ran with all my might. I ran and ran as hard as I could. I slipped a few times, but I kept running. I was in the lead with just about twenty yards from the top, but my three friends ran past me and were on the way to the top. Although I was tired, I told myself that I had to try my best to win, so I ran as fast as I could. And you know what?"

"What? What happened?" Kirabo pleaded as he anxiously implored Adamu to finish the story.

"I passed all of my friends and made it to the top first. I won."

"Wow, you must be fast."

The age difference between Adamu, who was now twenty, and the nine-year-old Kirabo was immaterial. Their friendship, which was more like a brotherhood, was a vital element that helped each get through the seconds of each day when the painful memories were always ready to fill their thoughts. While parts of their tattered souls would remain forever empty, the respite they were able to provide each other from those painful memories made the importance they held in each other's lives immeasurable.

Looking out at the soccer game, Kirabo dejectedly said, "Without my leg, I will never be able to make it to the top of a big hill. I will never be able to run or play again. Never."

Regretting that he told the story about his run up Lafon Hill, Adamu wished that he could tell Kirabo he was wrong and that he would be able to run and play again. But deep inside he thought that Kirabo was probably right. Like everything else, hope was a limited resource in the camp.

Standing behind the wheelchair, Adamu, who could not think of what to say, remained silent. When the boy dropped his head and began to cry, Adamu held him tightly around his shoulders.

Mile 7

After eating a plate of pasta with mozzarella and tomatoes big enough for practically three servings, William announced, "Another satisfying meal. I am stuffed. I can't eat anymore. What's for dessert?"

Christina laughed and said, "You know that void that you have been saying you wanted to fill? I don't think it can be filled with food."

"Oh, yeah? Watch me try," William said with a mischievous smile.

After finishing off two slices of apple pie with vanilla ice cream, William moved to the couch and took a seat next to Maggie, their Airedale terrier, who was taking a nap on the couch, which she technically was not allowed to be on. He grabbed the TV remote, used Maggie's back as an armrest, and flipped indiscriminately through the channels.

"Please, William. Stop. Pick a channel," Christina pleaded as she entered the living room and ordered Maggie off the couch.

William settled on a news channel where there was a report about the violent conflict occurring in Southern Sudan.

"This is so terrible. I have been reading about this in the paper."

The program went on to profile the plight and journey of a group of young male refugees from Southern Sudan dubbed "The Lost Boys" who had been forced out of their villages. The news story showed how, through the work of various agencies, some of the refugees were placed to live with families in the United States.

The families gave the young men not only food and shelter, but also a chance at a new life. All of the refugees profiled in the story were pleasant, kind, and genuinely decent people.

"We should do that," Christina declared.

"What?"

"Take one of those young men in."

"Yeah, right," William responded sarcastically.

"Really, I think it would be great. We would be giving someone a chance to have a life. At this stage in our life, we should give back. We have the opportunity to do it. And we certainly have the space. We have so much. We are so fortunate. We should look into it."

"Are you kidding?"

"No. I am serious, William. Think about it. You have been saying that you are looking for something in life. Here it is. You would be great for someone. We can give someone a chance to have a good life. Look at what those boys have been through. They need help. This can be good. I am telling you, this is what you have been looking for."

William thought about it. "Oh, I don't know."

"You would be such a good influence on someone. This would be good for you, and we would be helping someone out. Think about it."

Without responding, William hoisted himself off of the couch to graze in the kitchen for yet even more dessert.

While Christina's idea initially seemed radically far-fetched, William recognized long ago that her suggestions usually proved to be sound and merited thoughtful consideration. While in the kitchen he thought about how helping someone in need would be the right thing to do and how it was true that they certainly had the space and the resources to do it.

Before he even returned to the living room, he concluded that Christina's thought that they should open their home to a Lost Boy of Sudan was something they should have a long talk about.

Mile 8

Word spread quickly among the refugees. The United Nations and the international community had arranged for many of them to be placed in the United States.

To Adamu, it was not good news. He wanted to stay with Tahir and Kirabo and hoped he could eventually return to his village and reunite with his mother and sister. Although the refugee camp was far from a great solution, he had made many friends and did not want to be separated from them. The refugees had bonded and were able to bring a sense of community to the remote and secluded camp.

The life he had in Africa for all of his years of existence was all he knew. Leaving was not an option that Adamu could even begin to evaluate and consider.

"Adamu, I heard that they are posting a list today of who is getting picked to leave and where they are headed," Kirabo informed Adamu of something he was already fully aware of.

"Well, I am not going, even if I get picked. I want to return to my village one day. I will stay here," Adamu said definitively.

Adamu pushed Kirabo's wheelchair over to the center of the camp where the list of refugees, who would have the opportunity to leave, was going to be posted. A huge crowd surrounded the list as soon as it was tacked up on a bulletin board, and it was apparent that it would take a good amount of time before Adamu and Kirabo would be able to read it.

"Go ahead, Adamu. Look at the list. Leave me here," Kirabo said as they waited on the outskirts of the group in front of the bulletin board.

Adamu managed to fight through the crowd and made it to the three-page list. To the right of each name was a location where the selected refugee was to be placed if they consented.

Adamu ran his finger down the list as he looked out for his, Kirabo's, and Tahir's name. After getting through two and a half pages, he did not see any of the three names. Then he spotted one. It was his. Without looking to see where he could be placed, Adamu finished scanning the list for Kirabo's and Tahir's names. Neither was on the list. Adamu looked back up the list to his name and looked to the right of it. It said "Verona, Oregon, United States."

"What did it say?" Kirabo asked with great interest when Adamu returned.

"Neither of us is on the list. Neither is Tahir. We are all staying."

The badly damaged plastic bucket was partially buried in the dirt road. Dr. Zamora figured it had sunk into the dirt during the heavy rain days earlier and then a vehicle had driven over it; breaking it and burying it even deeper. Now that the ground was dry, the disfigured bucket was stuck. Dr. Zamora dug into the dirt with a small shovel and, with great effort, pulled and tugged the bucket until he successfully dislodged it.

He placed it upside down and cut it in half with a hacksaw. He then placed one half of the dismantled bucket on the ground and used the hacksaw to cut a curved piece of plastic about four inches wide and ten inches long from the top rim portion of the bucket.

After washing off the dirt and smoothing the edges, he wrapped the piece with layers of gauze, cotton balls, and surgical tape. The construction of the well-cushioned neck brace was finished.

Short on supplies and resources, Dr. Zamora used his ingenuity to provide the best care possible to the refugees. He put the newly constructed neck brace in the storage room and grabbed a pair of crutches. After adjusting the height of the crutches, he carried them out of the storage room.

"Kirabo, you are doing great. You are getting stronger and healing well," Dr. Zamora said as he approached him. "It is time to start using crutches."

Adamu helped the boy out of his wheelchair and held him as Kirabo nervously took hold of the handles on the crutches. Standing on his one and only foot, Kirabo wobbled as the cushioned part of each crutch pressed firmly into his underarms.

"You can do it, Kirabo. Stay on your foot and extend the crutches out forward a little, then swing your body up to meet them," Dr. Zamora instructed with encouragement.

Kirabo, who quickly became comfortable with his crutches, nimbly moved around the medical tent and stopped in front of Dr. Zamora and Adamu.

"Very good, Kirabo. Very good," Dr. Zamora said, smiling. Then turning to Adamu, he asked, "So, Adamu, have you decided to go to America?"

The secret that Adamu had been keeping for days was out.

Shocked, wide-eyed Kirabo looked at Adamu and said, "America? You said that you weren't on the list. You got chosen to go?"

Adamu let out a deep breath and said, "Kirabo, I don't want to go, so I told you that I was not on the list."

"This is a great opportunity for you. Why don't you want to go?" Dr. Zamora asked.

"I want to stay here. With my friends, with you, Kirabo. I want to return to my village one day. I want to find my mother and sister."

The doctor said, "Adamu, I understand. But this is a great opportunity for you. I think you should take advantage of it."

"Dr. Zamora, why should I have the chance to go when others are more deserving? How come Kirabo can't go? I already told the officials that they should let him go instead of me."

"Adamu, this is not a matter of being deserving or not. A number of factors are considered. Kirabo cannot go. He is still being treated. They are going to try to place as many people as they can. The ones not on the list will be considered in the future. I think that you should reconsider your decision. This is your chance."

Although he would miss his friend terribly if he left, Kirabo, the small boy who could not even manage to smile, found the courage and strength to put his own interests aside.

Holding onto his crutches tightly, he looked deeply into Adamu's eyes.

"I would miss you, but you should go. This chance is a gift from the Creator. My father always said that if you were fortunate enough to receive such a gift, you should accept it. You should cherish such a gift and make the most out of it. Adamu, go to America."

The plane rumbled down the bumpy dirt runway picking up more speed along the way as Adamu pressed back into his seat and held onto the belt across his lap. When it appeared to Adamu that the plane could not go any faster, the sound of the jets intensified and, with a surge of power, the plane had lift-off.

It was difficult to leave, but Tahir, Dr. Zamora, and Kirabo had convinced him to go. He was torn, but he concluded that if the people he loved and respected felt so strongly that he should go to America, he should follow their advice.

His reluctance to leave the refugee camp, and the pain and loss he had endured, left Adamu feeling somewhat unfazed by his first experience with flight. Instead of being scared or excited, he felt next to nothing. Along with so many other things he had lost since the attack on his village, Adamu had lost a good amount of his ability to feel.

From his vantage point in the sky, Africa looked peaceful and more beautiful than he had ever realized.

He yearned for his mother and sister as he thought they must be somewhere in the vast land spread out for miles below.

Although unsure, he thought that he spotted Lafon Hill far off in the distance. He thought about the moment he stood on top of the hill with his friends and remembered what Salim said that last day when all was good: *"We will always be able to say that we did it together."*

As he was being shuttled through the sky, leaving the continent where he had spent his whole life and into an unknown future, Adamu's thoughts were filled with what he had lost and what he was leaving behind.

His tears proved that he had not totally lost all of his ability to feel.

The frigid, unwelcoming Oregon air greeted Adamu as soon as he stepped off the plane onto the retractable walkway leading to the gate.

Weary from his travels on four different airplanes, and emotional from leaving Africa, the warm and welcoming smiles on the faces of the people holding a sign with his name on it was not enough for him to feel comfortable in the cold and unfamiliar new surroundings.

"Hello, Adamu. I am Christina, and this is William. Welcome to Oregon. We are so happy that you are going to share our home with us," Christina said as she hugged the thin young man with sad eyes. During the embrace she could feel the frailness of Adamu's body and sense the weakness of his spirit. Adamu said hello and weakly shook William's hand.

Seeing that Adamu was just wearing sandals, thin slacks, and a thin long-sleeved shirt, William took off his jacket and placed it around his shoulders to keep him warm. Then he took hold of the small plastic bag Adamu was holding, which amounted to his entire luggage, and the three walked to the car.

Having been informed of Adamu's height, weight, and shoe size, Christina had purchased a few sets of new clothes and footwear for Adamu before his arrival. The Caldwell's also worked hard to clean and organize Nicholas' old room for Adamu. William also had arranged that, after Adamu got settled, he could start working part-time three days a week in the mailroom at his law firm. Christina and William thought that the job would help him to meet people and assimilate to life in Oregon.

During the first few weeks after his arrival, Christina brought Adamu with her when she went shopping and ran errands. Like the good school teacher she was, Christina used each excursion as an opportunity to teach him about the customs and practices in the United States.

She was routinely struck by Adamu's good-natured innocence, generosity, and strong values. Adamu was accepting of all people he met, and most everyone took an immediate liking to him.

Christina told William that she felt Adamu was teaching her more than she was teaching him.

Adamu was one of the lucky Sudanese refugees who was placed with a family in the United States. His journey to establish his life in a new country had fewer obstacles and was far easier than the majority of other refugees. Most of the Lost Boys were set up to live with three or four other refugees in an apartment, and were required to work and to pay their bills.

While they were provided with orientation services, which helped them find employment, housing, and taught them about life in the United States, for the most part they were on their own. It was sink or swim, and they had to fend for themselves. They worked low-paying and tough jobs, and they had to scratch and claw to make it. Many worked multiple jobs.

Adamu's placement with the Caldwell's was like a child who was fortunate to be born into a financially sound and loving family in an ideal community. He was certainly lucky to be placed with William and Christina.

Like other Lost Boys, Adamu had difficulty comprehending and accepting the notion of securing his financial stability before helping others.

During the orientation process, the Lost Boys were advised to be sure to pay their rent and bills, and to try to build a savings reserve, before giving money that they earned to others.

In Sudan, things were shared and there was not a focus on accumulating individual material wealth; in fact, it was frowned upon. As such, Adamu and many other Lost Boys routinely ignored the advice to secure their own financial stability before helping others.

Especially in the first few months of being placed in the United States, many of the Lost Boys would send a high percentage of the money they earned to their friends and family.

While they certainly had a tough life in the United States and had little disposable income, many Lost Boys felt an obligation to help others they knew were suffering.

Christina, who helped Adamu set up a savings and checking account, became aware of his generosity when helping him balance his checkbook. She discovered that he was using most of his earnings from working at William's law firm to send items to Kirabo, Tahir, and others still in the refugee camp.

In an effort to help him learn that he needed to be more conservative in his generosity, Christina prepared a monthly budget and included items on it that Adamu would be responsible for when he eventually moved out. She tried to help him realize that he needed to take steps to ensure his own financial stability.

Nevertheless, when his savings account increased to a modest amount, Adamu battled with feelings that he was selfishly hoarding money.

Mile 9

Christina moved the bowl of millet powder mixed with water, which she prepared in the morning, to the back of the counter. Then she opened a cookbook of African food she recently bought at the bookstore and read the instructions again for *kajaik,* which was described as a stew popular in Sudan. Outside of just a few meals, Christina did not think that Adamu liked any of the food she had been serving. Adamu was so skinny she feared that he was not eating enough.

When she overheard a reporter on the television that Adamu was watching in the living room mention Sudan, she stopped preparing the food and listened more closely. The reporter was recounting the ongoing atrocities in Southern Sudan; the same atrocities that Adamu had experienced.

Christina walked slowly to the doorway of the kitchen and looked out into the living room. Adamu was sitting on the edge of the couch, facing the television with his back to her. She could see the disturbing images on the television as the reporter talked about the *"dead and displaced,"* the *"burned out villages,"* the *"ethnic cleansing,"* and the *"Lost Boys of Sudan."*

Christina stood frozen. She wanted to run into the room and turn the television off, but at the same time, she knew that he had a right to watch.

Her heart ached as she watched Adamu slide off the couch, drop to his knees, and inch closer to the television. As the television showed footage of destroyed villages, Adamu reached out and touched the television screen.

Christina slowly retreated into the kitchen. She cried quietly as she heard Adamu sobbing in the other room. When she heard Adamu leave the living room and head upstairs to the solitude of Nicholas' old room, she allowed her cries to become louder.

Seeing Adamu's pain firsthand was the motivating factor for Christina to become even more involved in helping the Lost Boys. She offered advice to other families planning to open their homes to a refugee, worked to provide resources to the many refugees who were not placed with a family, and helped set up a social network where the refugees in the United States could get in touch with each other as a means of support. She was very excited about her role in helping with the arrangements for a weekend where hundreds of Lost Boys from across the country would get together.

But above all, Christina's most heartfelt efforts were dedicated to keeping in touch with United Nations representatives from various refugee camps in Kenya and Ethiopia in an effort to find information about Adamu's mother and sister. The pain in Adamu's eyes caused by what had happened to his family, and Christina's understanding of the love of family, required her to act. Not wanting to provide Adamu with any false hope or added stress, she kept her efforts to locate his mother and sister a secret.

Christina stepped away from the meal she was preparing, wiped her hands with a towel, dried her tears with a tissue, looked at the clock, and figured out what time it was in Ethiopia. Desperate to find Adamu's mother and sister with the hope that they could reunite with Adamu, she opened up her notebook and dialed the long phone number of one of the United Nations representatives whom she had already spoken with on numerous occasions.

An hour or so later, Adamu came back down stairs to the living room. As he petted Maggie, Christina brought out an armful of photo albums, dropped them on the coffee table, and sat on the couch near Adamu.

Christina was trying her best to get him to think about anything other than his pain and losses even for a moment.

"Adamu, these are some photo albums of our family over the years. You have to take a look at them; they are fun to look at." As they went through the albums together, Christina discussed the back stories of the photos. After they finished looking at one, Adamu picked up another, which had a picture of William on the front.

"Oh, that is a great one, Adamu," Christina said. "The kids and I put it together for William as a gift for his 50th birthday."

The album chronicled William's life with pictures and mementos that spanned from his birth to his 50th birthday. In addition to pictures, it also contained other things, such as ticket stubs and receipts, which recorded events in William's life.

The last picture in the album was a family picture taken at William's 50th birthday party.

Adamu liked looking through the album; he could tell that the Caldwell's were good people who cared about each other. When Adamu was up to the pages documenting William's high school years, William returned home from work.

"Hey, guys. What's happening?" William asked loudly as he walked through the door and worked to undo the tie around his neck.

"Hi, William," Adamu said, "We are looking at you."

"I am showing Adamu some of the photo albums. We are looking through the one we gave you on your 50th birthday."

"Oh, that's a great one. Are you up to my post-200 pound years yet?" William asked jokingly as he sat down next to Adamu to look at the album with him.

"Look at that skinny guy, Adamu," William said as he pointed to a picture of himself when he was a freshman in high school running at a track meet.

Adamu asked, "You were on a team?"

"Yeah, I was on the track team in high school and college. I used to be a runner a long time ago." Then William boastfully added, "A pretty decent one too, I might add."

William flipped a few pages forward and excitedly said, "Look at this; this is me in college."

On one page was a big picture of William in his running uniform of gray shorts with maroon stripes on the side and a maroon tank top with grey trim and the word "Bradford" in bold white lettering. William was young, lean, and had long hair.

"Wow, look at that guy, Adamu!" William was amazed and proud of what he once was.

On the next page was a group picture of William with his team and coach. A large trophy was on the ground, and everyone was smiling. William was on the far right side of the photo but, unlike his teammates, he was not in uniform.

William was standing on crutches.

"That's the 1974 championship team for Bradford. These are my teammates and that's Coach Bellinger," William said as he pointed out some of the people in the photo. "All great guys. I couldn't run in the championship tournament. I got hurt weeks before. That was the end of my running career. I missed the entire tournament."

William pulled up the left pant leg of his suit pants to show Adamu the long and raised scar from the surgery he underwent in college. "That was done before they perfected knee surgery. Nowadays there would not be a scar like that after a surgery for the type of injury I had."

Although William was smiling in the photo, whenever he looked at it, he recalled how disappointed he had felt at the time. Despite the years that had passed, it was a feeling that still resonated. The injury he sustained in practice prevented him from being a part of the team when it actually won the championship. He had worked so hard from freshman year on to help build a winning team, and he just missed out on being part of the championship.

Whenever he recalled his time on the Bradford track team, disappointment and emptiness, due to his injury, always surfaced along with the happy memories.

"Anyway, things happen, but boy, was that a fun time. It was great. I loved running and being part of the team."

“I love running too,” Adamu said with meaning as he turned to William. William recognized it was one of the few times that Adamu offered anything to him or Christina about his life and interests.

“Really? Yeah, running is great.” After a brief pause, William asked, “Hey, would you like me to show you a great place to run sometime?”

“Okay,” Adamu said with a slight smile.

“Okay, great.” William was overjoyed because he saw Adamu open up just a little. In an effort to seal the deal, William quickly added “This weekend.”

Although he had not run in years, he jumped at the opportunity to do something with Adamu that they might enjoy together.

Mile 10

On Saturday morning, William drove his old Volvo station wagon twenty minutes over to a local county park. Because of the large number of ducks that called the pond in the park home, most locals referred to it as "Duck Park."

Besides the pond, Duck Park had a picnic area, a playground, a dog run, as well as a paved trail. The trail, which meandered through wooded areas, open fields, and over a few picturesque bridges, was ideal for running. Markers were placed alongside the trail at every tenth of a mile, which allowed people to know how much they walked, biked, or ran. The trail went out three miles, so a full circuit would be six miles.

However, on this day, William had no intention of seeing any marker beyond the one mile mark, and he would have no problem turning back before then.

Although it had been years since he had worn a pair of running sneakers for their intended use, William was excited to do something with Adamu that might help him feel more comfortable in his new surroundings.

Still not acclimated to the cold climate of Oregon, Adamu was heavily bundled up.

He was wearing two pairs of sweatpants, three sweat shirts—one with a hood—a knit hat, and large gloves. The pair of new running sneakers that William and Christina bought him fit snuggly over two pairs of socks.

He was by far the most heavily dressed runner in the park.

As the two jogged slowly, their conversation was more comfortable than it had ever been. Running together in the clean, crisp air helped to dissolve any walls or apprehension between them. The beginning of a bond of friendship and understanding was being formed with each stride as they exchanged stories.

Adamu laughed at the story William told about how their dog, Maggie once got chased in the park by a bunch of Canadian geese, and Adamu told William about how he and his friends would play various games and run together in Sudan.

When they completed one mile, William, who was surprised that he had made it that far, kept running. He was enjoying being with Adamu and seeing him open up.

It also felt good to do a little running.

After a few more minutes, William felt he had reached his limit. In between breaths he said, "Adamu, keep going, I am holding you back...I had enough...I am going to turn around and walk...I will be at the car...Keep going."

"Are you sure? Come on, you could do more."

"No, that's it for me. I haven't run in years. If I go any further I don't think I will have enough in me to get back," he said as he felt a pain in his right hip. "Keep going, have fun."

Adamu said "Okay" and then ran off on the trail, which veered to the right into a wooded area.

After Adamu ran off, William decided to keep jogging a little bit further; although at a slower pace.

He figured he should try to run at least to the one and a half mile mark and that, if he made it, he would earn a nice slow walk back to the car.

While jogging he took in the beauty of the park. The colors of the leaves of the trees were illuminated brightly by the sun. It was a great, clear day—a perfect day to be out on a run.

A group of kids were playing soccer in the large grass field, and cyclists, runners, and walkers of all ages were enjoying the trail.

Far off in the distance ahead, William could see the paved trail run perpendicular for a stretch. As he was about to turn around to walk back to the car, he noticed something out of the corner of his eye on the trail off in the distance. It was an object that was moving from his right to left. He squinted his eyes. He thought it was a cyclist riding by, but he realized it was a runner. He recognized the clothes. It was Adamu.

To say that Adamu was jogging would not be a fair characterization—it was more like he was gliding. William stood and watched in awe as Adamu ran for about fifty yards before the trail veered off, and he disappeared into another wooded area. Despite the fact that Adamu was wearing many layers of clothes, William had a thought that Adamu might be one of the most graceful runners he had ever seen.

When William was almost back at the start of the trail, Adamu ran up alongside and slowed to a walk.

"Hey, William," Adamu said excitedly.

"Hey, Adamu. Do you like the park?"

"Oh, I love it, I love it. All the trees, the animals, and the people. It is really great," he said beaming. William recognized it was the first time that Adamu seemed truly happy and comfortable since he had arrived in Oregon.

The decision to go running was a success.

"Yeah, it is really great to live near this park. Hey, I saw you running. You were running really great."

Adamu smiled and said, "This place is great. I really like the waterfall."

In shock, William stopped walking and said in disbelief, "Adamu, the waterfall is at the end of the trail. It's at the three mile marker. You made it all the way to the three mile mark and back?"

Sensing William's amazement, Adamu proclaimed excitedly, "Yes. I saw the waterfall!"

"No way. You saw the waterfall? You ran to the three mile marker?"

"Yes! I saw the number three sign too." Adamu said, laughing while clapping. Then he added, "I saw the waterfall. With the rocks all around it. And the benches where the people sit."

The further description of the three mile mark was enough corroborating evidence to convince the lawyer that Adamu did indeed make it to the end of the trail and back. William was flabbergasted. Adamu had run the entire trail. William tried to figure out how fast Adamu must have run, but he could not calculate it. He concluded, *"Either this kid is gifted or I walked really slowly on the way back to the car—or both."*

That night William excitedly retold the story of the day in the park with Adamu to Christina for the fourth time. He was energized that Adamu was really happy, and he told his wife how great it made him feel to see Adamu open up.

As William finally settled into bed, he knew it was going to be one of those nights where he would have trouble falling asleep.

His mind was racing about work-related issues and about the breakthrough with Adamu.

After he could tell that Christina fell asleep, William slowly got out of bed and, in an effort to avoid the creaky spots, gingerly walked across the wood floor and left the bedroom.

On his way to the kitchen, William walked past Nicholas' old room. The lights in the room were off, but William could hear Adamu crying. As he listened, William's excitement about the run in the park earlier in the day disappeared as he was reminded that Adamu was still hurting.

As he sat in the kitchen, drinking wine and eating pieces of French bread with mozzarella, William recognized he would need to take it slow with Adamu. He knew that, while there may be some breakthrough moments and some good times, it would be a long, slow process.

With guidance and support, he hoped he could help give Adamu more moments, like earlier in the day, where the pain could be pushed to the back burner, for just a little bit at least.

Mile 11

Over the next month and a half, William and Adamu went running in Duck Park several days a week. William would never be running that much, but seeing how Adamu really enjoyed it, he made an effort to join him. William was re-discovering running too. His old love of the sport was being rekindled after a very long slumber. He was up to running five miles—a distance he had not run in decades, and he even lost ten pounds since his first run with Adamu.

Although he still did not like the cold weather, Adamu loved being outside. When he ran, he took notice of everything—kids playing games he never saw before, rabbits in the brush, the ducks in the stream alongside the trail. Adamu even pointed things out to William that he had never noticed before. During their runs it was clear Adamu was a talented runner. His form was flawless, and he moved like the wind without showing a hint of exertion or fatigue.

While William was extremely interested in finding out how fast his young gifted houseguest could run, Adamu seemed to have no interest in knowing. He was just running for sheer enjoyment.

On a few occasions, William had Adamu wear his stopwatch in an effort to time him, but each attempt proved to be a colossal failure due to operator error—the operator being Adamu.

The first time Adamu wore the stopwatch, they decided to run to the two mile mark and back, a four mile run. When William finished, he quickly ran over to Adamu, who finished earlier, to check his time. When Adamu held up the watch, William saw that it was still running—Adamu had forgotten to stop it when he finished.

When he saw the watch William said, "Hey, not bad—not bad for me—you didn't stop the watch when you finished. That's my time!" Adamu just smiled and laughed.

On another occasion, Adamu must have hit the start/stop button twice at the very beginning of the run and forgot to hit it again when he finished, so the time of Adamu's four mile run was 1.22 seconds. When William saw the time he said, "Adamu, I know you are fast, but this is ridiculous...1.22 seconds!" Again, Adamu just laughed.

As refreshing as Adamu's approach to running was, William was going crazy trying to figure out how fast he was.

While leafing through the newspaper one day, he felt he found the perfect solution. A 10K charity race was being held in a nearby town in two weeks. Although he had yet to run over five miles, William was up for the challenge—especially if it meant that Adamu would be timed.

Adamu happily agreed to participate when William suggested they do it together.

Christina was in the kitchen getting ingredients organized for making dinner when Nicholas called from New York.

As William walked into the kitchen, he overheard the conversation and he excitedly tugged on Christina's shirt like a little kid as he asked if Nicholas was coming home for his break from school.

She smiled at him and nodded her head up and down, as she continued to speak on the phone, "Okay, so you are going to see Jessica in Seattle for few days and then you will be coming here on the 25th. Landing here at 8:45 in the morning. That is just great, we are so excited. Adamu is really looking forward to meeting you."

Over dinner William realized that Nicholas was scheduled to land in Oregon on the same morning the 10K race was scheduled.

He always picked up Nicholas at the airport, and he would cancel pretty much anything to do it. Disappointed by the conflict, he said, "I'll pass on the run and pick Nicholas up, but Adamu, you should still do it."

Christina quickly responded, "William, do the race. I can pick Nicholas up. You and Adamu have been running together for a while now, and you should both do the race. In fact, because he is landing at 8:45, I can pick him up, and we can go straight to the race and watch you guys run. How about that?"

Yet again, Christina had found a solution to a problem.

Enthusiastic runners of various ages and ability milled about before the start of the 10K.

Lining up for an organized race for the first time since he was on the Bradford track team, William thought about how the local runs he participated in as a youth had dramatically influenced his life in a positive way.

Besides being a lot of fun, running in races as a middle-school-aged kid helped him form a love for the sport, which continued through high school. His high school track success led him to Bradford, which, in turn, provided him with the opportunity to meet Christina, have a wonderful family, and a good solid career.

Standing next to a few teenagers getting prepared to run, he chuckled to himself when he realized that, even though it was just a fun event, he was feeling the same anxious nervousness he had felt before races decades earlier.

"A little nervousness is a good thing," he told himself. "Are you ready Adamu?"

"I am ready," Adamu said, with a big smile.

"Well, I'm ready…to finally find out how fast you are," William said with a prideful smile as if he, at last, had figured out how to solve the mystery of the universe.

A man excitedly shouted over a loud speaker: "On your mark, get set….go!" and the race began.

Adamu, who was off in a flash, joined a small group of talented runners at the front, which quickly separated from the majority of the other runners. After Adamu and the other lead runners disappeared from his sight around a bend in the road, William focused on running his best.

While it was a fun event, he brought a level of seriousness to it. He had been running consistently for the past few months, and he wanted to have a strong run.

His desire to compete had returned.

The 10K route was considered "an out and back" course, which meant that the runners would run to about the 5K point, turn around on the same road, and return to the finish line, which also served as the start.

William was finding the course, which had a few hills, to be pretty challenging. As early as a mile into the race, he began to feel fatigued. After feeling a strong burning sensation in his thighs, he realized that his recent running on the flat trails in Duck Park failed to include any hills.

When he reached a welcome flat portion of the course, he could tell the hills took a lot out of him, and he did not have the energy he expected. He also realized he had started out too fast and was paying for it. While discouraged, he took note that he would need to incorporate some hill work in his future training runs.

The fact that he was planning new training strategies was a clear indication that the athlete within him was truly re-awakening.

As he tried to regain a positive approach, William heard the runners near him suddenly start clapping. He quickly realized that they were clapping for Adamu who was the leader of the run on the other side of the street heading to the finish line. William was excited to see that Adamu was in the lead and was touched that the other runners would use some of their energy to encourage him on to the finish.

Adamu spotted him on the other side of the street and yelled out, "Hey, William!"

William pumped his fist in the air and yelled back, "Go, Adamu, go."

Adamu's smile was as bright as could be as the two passed by each other. Adamu had a gigantic lead; it took almost a full minute for the next runner trailing him to pass William.

As he continued his run, William was filled with pride and was overjoyed that Adamu was happy and running a great race. He was also looking forward to learning Adamu's time—he was finally going to find out how fast Adamu really was.

The route curved to the right, and when he saw the finish line straight ahead about a half a mile away, William tried his best to increase the power in his fatigued legs in an effort to shave as many seconds he could off of his finishing time.

Spectators standing behind metal railings lining the course clapped and yelled out words of encouragement to the runners.

With just two tenths of a mile to the finish line, William saw Adamu on the left side of the course, smiling and waving his arms wildly as he stood next to Christina, Nicholas, and Maggie who were behind the metal railings.

Confused that Adamu was still on the course, William stopped running when he reached them to investigate.

He gave his son a quick hug over the metal railing, turned to Adamu and hurriedly asked, "Did you finish?"

Because Adamu was too slow to respond, he turned to Christina and Nicholas and asked, "Did he finish? Tell me he finished."

"No, he spotted us and stopped to say hi to Nicholas. We told him to keep going, but he wouldn't go," Christina said as she threw her hands up and gave a look that said, *"We did all we could, but he would not listen."* William was frustrated, upset, and amused all at the same time. Again, he would have to wait to find out how fast Adamu could actually run.

Despite his love for his son, even William would not have stopped on the course to say hi if he was on his way to a win; it was a race after all.

William looked at Adamu and asked in disbelief "You didn't finish? You had the race in the bag." Adamu just smiled and laughed. With a laugh William shook his head, and said "Unbelievable. C'mon, let's stop chit chatting. We have a run to finish," and the two ran off to complete the last part of the race together.

When they approached the finish line, Adamu stopped and gave William a playful push forward, and William officially finished before Adamu.

On their way back to meet up with Christina and Nicholas, thunderous applause erupted among the spectators. William and Adamu stopped to take notice and realized that the cheers were for a sixty-three-year-old man who was sprinting the final stretch of the race.

A regular in the local running scene, with highly defined calf muscles and marathon medals to prove it, the man could hear the cheers, but could not see the crowd.

Holding one end of a long piece of cloth, while his guide running beside him held the other, the blind runner was digging deep to try to set a new personal record in the 10K.

As many in the crowd shouted out, *"Go Achilles!"* William and Adamu joined in the cheers as they watched his inspired push to the finish.

When his guide told him that he had met his goal of setting a personal record, he raised his arms in celebration and waved in all directions to thank the supportive crowd. He was soon engulfed in hugs from his teammates on the Achilles track club.

Adamu congratulated the runner when he walked by, "Great job, sir."

Stopping to talk, the man said, "Yeah, thanks. I had a good day out there today. I have to keep it up because I'm training for a marathon."

Because he had never heard of a marathon before, Adamu asked, "What is a marathon?"

"It is exactly the length of this race plus twenty more miles—26.2 miles."

"Twenty more miles! Wow!"

"You could do it too," the man said with an encouraging smile as he patted Adamu on the shoulder.

Pizza boxes and trays of pasta from Renato's Pizzeria filled the dinner table. It was a party of sorts to welcome Nicholas home and to celebrate William and Adamu's achievements on the racecourse.

"Dad, really, you look like you lost weight. I have not seen you in a couple of months; I can tell. It is great that you are out there running. Great job, Adamu, for getting him off the couch," Nicholas said as he and Adamu, who had instantly connected, exchanged a high five.

"Thanks. But I think that I will happily put some weight back on with this meal," William said as he dished some cheese ravioli onto his plate and picked up a slice of pizza with extra sauce out of the box.

"So tell us more about NYU and New York. How are your classes going?" Christina asked Nicholas for probably the one-hundredth time since he had left for school.

"It is really great. I love it. My classes are really cool. Everyone in the film department is so talented. I am learning so much from my teachers and from my classmates. And I just love New York. The energy of the city is incredible," he said as he handed Adamu a plate of spaghetti with meatballs.

"New York sounds like a nice place. I would like to see it one day," Adamu said.

"Yeah, definitely. You have to visit. You could stay in my dorm. We would have the best time. I will show you all around. Maybe the next time I have a break you could come out."

Adamu smiled and nodded his head in agreement. He was happy he had made a new friend in Nicholas.

In between bites of his meal, Adamu told Christina and Nicholas, "We met a blind man who ran in the race today. He was amazing. He said that he is going to run a long distance race called a marathon soon."

"Wait. I have an idea!" Nicholas announced excitedly as he turned to his dad. "You and Adamu are runners now. You both should do the New York City Marathon. I watched the marathon last year and it is amazing. Yes, that is perfect. You can all come to New York and stay for a while. It would be great." Nicholas turned to Adamu and the two exchanged another high five.

"A marathon? No way. I can't run a marathon," William protested. Then he added, "26.2 miles? That's crazy. I barely finished the 10K today. My legs were weak by the three mile mark. There is no way I could have run another twenty miles today."

"Well, honey, you could work up to it. You just have to train for it," Christina said as a sly smile crossed over her face.

"Yeah Dad, you could do it. What are you talking about, *'I can't?'* You are the one who always told me not to say *'I can't'* do something. And for how long have I heard you say that you were a top runner in high school and college? Prove it. Come on. You could do it."

William looked around the room. Everyone was smiling except him.

He was outnumbered. Everyone was already signed on to the idea that he run a marathon.

He was the only one holding back.

"Oh, I don't know. That is a lot of miles. I did not run anything close to a marathon in high school or college. I ran the 1500 meters. The most that I probably ever ran at one time was 15 miles and that was literally decades ago—before you were even born, Nicholas. I am too old for all that now. I am past my prime," he contended. He could tell his argument was not persuading anyone. He meekly added, "Oh, I don't know."

"Come on, Dad. You could do it. It would be great. You have a ton of time to train. Adamu could see New York. We would have a great time together."

Christina chimed in, "I think that you could do it, honey, it would be good for you."

"Well, maybe."

"Yeah! That's a yes. You are going to do it!" Nicholas triumphantly declared.

"I said maybe. I did not say yes. I will consider it. Here is the thing. If I can get up to 15 miles within two months, and if I could lose ten more pounds, I will strongly consider it. How's that?"

"No, you won't *strongly consider* it. You *will* do it. Adamu, you are on your way to New York," Nicholas said as the two exchanged another high five.

As they were getting ready for bed, Christina and William talked about how great the day had turned out.

"I am so happy to see Adamu and Nicholas together," Christina said. "They really get along great. You could really see a different side of Adamu when he is with Nicholas. They seem like lifelong friends."

"Yeah, it is really great, but boy, I am in trouble with this marathon thing. It is really a lot of miles. I don't know if I can hold up over that distance. I'm too old for that."

"Of course, you can. People older than you do it. You can do it. Remember a few months ago when you were saying you had nothing to do and were in a funk? Well, look at you now. You are helping Adamu. You got back into running. And now you are going to do a marathon."

"I'm not *definitely* doing the marathon," William tried to clarify.

Without taking a breath to consider William's interjection, Christina continued, "Even though it will take a lot of time and training, it will be fun. It will bring you and Adamu even closer. You'll get into even better shape. There is plenty of time to train. You will do great."

"Oh, I don't know. A marathon is a daunting task. I can't believe I agreed to consider it. I really put myself in a tough spot. What did I get myself into?"

"Get some sleep. You are in training now," Christina said with a laugh as she turned out the light.

Mile 12

Standing in front of the kitchen sink, with the palm of his left hand on the counter providing balance, the man, who was closer to senior citizen status than middle age, arched his head back and finished his cup of instant coffee. He no longer found real enjoyment in the consumption of the beverage. It had been a long time since he had enjoyed a cup of coffee in the way it should—in the company of loved ones and friends over good conversation.

After placing the mug in the sink, he picked up a plastic plate, which had contained his microwave dinner from the night before. He ran it under the water for a few seconds to wash away the remnants of the bland and uninspired meal and tossed it in the overflowing recycle bin on the floor.

The disheveled apartment, his dwelling place for the last three years, was furnished with what could fit from the home he had shared with his wife for over thirty years. Unopened boxes from the move still littered the tiny apartment, which, in his mind, could never be considered home.

Besides the obvious size and style mismatches between the furniture and the small garden apartment, the man felt the furniture was out of place. It should be in his house. But those days were gone. Everything had changed after his wife passed on four years earlier.

He had nothing. The pain that he and his wife had to deal with when they learned they could not have children was unmercifully amplified now that he was alone. He had a few friends he spoke with on the phone once in a while, and occasionally met with them, but they all had lives and big families; he was alone. There was too much time that was unaccounted for in a given day, week, month, and year. Figuring out what to do with his time was the issue.

He knew he had a great life, but he did not feel that he *still* had one. His life was successful. He had achieved and enjoyed most everything that he had hoped for. But now it was like he had won the game, but somehow there was still time on the clock—and he was the only one on the playing field. He regretted not retiring earlier so that he could have spent more time with his wife, but he had no idea that she would get sick and be gone so soon.

Because he felt like he had no reason to put an effort into keeping the apartment clean, the bed was never made, blankets were never folded, shoes were never put away, and coats were never hung up. His old bike, and other things which should have been in a garage, were in the living room. Dinners with his wife were special times. Now it was just him and the microwave. Plates were rarely used. Eating out of a pizza box or the circular container the pasta would be delivered in sufficed. The television filled the silence.

Now that he was in a rental, everything seemed like a rental, including his life. People told him to move on, but he longed to go back. Memories, even the good ones, would bring the sadness.

Sadness had become his only companion, and he was getting far too comfortable with it.

As he began to doze off on the couch, the phone rang. After the third ring he found some initiative, rolled himself over, and answered the call.

In an official sounding voice, the person calling asked, "Hi, can I speak with Mr. Paul Bellinger please?"

Sensing that the person calling was a tele-marketer, he abruptly asked, "Who's calling?"

"My name is William Caldwell. I was a member of Mr. Bellinger's track team at Bradford back in the early '70s. I was hoping to get in touch with him."

The old coach, who had coached hundreds of kids over the years, ran the name through his mind. *"William Caldwell, William Caldwell,"* he said to himself. It registered.

"William Caldwell, the 1500 meters right?"

"That's right, coach. Wow, you remember! It is so good to hear your voice. I hope that I'm not catching you at a bad time."

"No, not at all. How are you doing William? How has everything been since Bradford?"

"Oh, everything is good. After Bradford I went to law school, got married, and had two kids. I've lived in Verona for the past twenty years or so and work in Elmsford. My daughter got married two years ago and lives in Seattle, and my son is in college in New York. So things have quieted down a bit."

"Good to hear it. It sure sounds like you have been busy since Bradford."

"So are you still coaching?"

"Oh, no. No more coaching, no more teaching. I have been put out to pasture. After I left Bradford, I coached at Oregon State for a good stretch, then I went over to Leonia High, where I coached and taught social studies. But since I retired it has been pretty quiet."

"So, coach, I am calling with a long story, but I will try to keep it short. My wife and I took in a young man named Adamu who is a refugee from Southern Sudan. There is a lot of political upheaval and violence going on there and thousands of people have been forced out of their own country. An agency placed a lot of the refugees in the United States." Without taking a breath, William continued, "So, because our kids are out of the house, we decided to take Adamu in. He is really a great kid who went through a very tough time. Some of his family members were killed, his village was destroyed, and he was beaten pretty bad."

"Oh, boy, that's terrible. That is great of you to take him in."

"Yeah, but it has been wonderful for us. He is really a fine young man. So this is why I am calling. One day he said that he liked running, so we went down to Duck Park for a jog, and I saw this kid run. Let me tell you coach, I never saw anything like it. He runs like the wind with great form. He really has a talent on another level. When he came to Oregon, he was clearly traumatized and having a tough time adjusting. The running is helping him feel more comfortable. My son came up with the idea that Adamu and I run the New York City Marathon in November and I agreed. I've been trying my best to give him some training tips, but there is only so much I can teach him. Hell, I need some instruction myself."

The old coach knew where this was going.

William continued, "I know he would benefit tremendously if someone like you could give him a little bit of formal training. So what do you think?"

"Oh, I don't know, William. I have been out of coaching for a while. I couldn't be much help."

"Listen, you would be great. I know it. You are a great coach. It would not be anything too serious. Just meet with him, watch him run, give him some advice."

"Oh, I don't know."

"I would be happy to pay you, of course," William added.

"That wouldn't be necessary. That's not it. I just don't know if I could be much help." In reality, since his wife had passed, he did not have the interest or energy to do much of anything.

William interrupted, "Coach, you'd be great. I really think this kid has a super talent. It would be a waste if it was not nurtured. I don't have the experience or know-how to help him harness his talent. I am telling you, this kid is special. I wouldn't be asking you if I didn't see something in him. He turned twenty-one a week before he arrived and I think he has the talent to have a promising future in the sport. I can't train with him on most days. And you would really be helping me out too. I need some instruction. I really don't know where to begin with training for a marathon. Plus, I would love to see you after all these years."

"Okay, I'll help you guys out."

"Great. I appreciate it. How about this Saturday morning at the Verona High School track?"

"Sure, I can get there."

"Okay, how about ten o'clock?"

"Sounds good."

Then, in a habit he had picked up over the years practicing as a lawyer, William re-stated the agreement clearly so that there would be no misunderstandings: "Saturday, ten o'clock a.m., Verona High track."

"Right, right. I'll be there."

After hanging up the phone, the old coach made himself another cup of instant coffee. As the hours and days after the call with William passed, he found himself looking forward to Saturday.

For the first time in a long while, he had plans to do something on the weekend.

Mile 13

"It is very good. Thank you," Adamu said, after he swallowed the first spoonful of *acidah,* a thick Sudanese maize that Christina made him for breakfast. While Christina, who worked hard at trying to make Adamu feel at home, was not sure if he was just being polite, she did have a feeling that the quality and authenticity of her Sudanese cooking was improving.

Like William, she recognized that, in spite of his pleasant personality, Adamu was still hurting. Being mindful of not trying to force too much on him, she lovingly and thoughtfully took measures, and planned future efforts, to help make Adamu feel more comfortable.

"Oh, great, Adamu. I hope that the *acidah* will give you some energy for your running today with William's old coach," she said as she poured herself a cup of coffee and sat next to him at the table.

"Adamu, I have something for you. I know you like looking at the photo albums of our family, so I got one for you." Christina reached over and picked up a big book from the chair next to her and slid it across the table.

Placing his hands on the soft blue cover with gold trim, Adamu smiled, "Thank you. Thank you."

"Open it, Adamu. I already started it for you."

Adamu opened to the first page and saw two pictures, secured under a clear sheet. In one photo, Adamu was bundled up in a heavy winter coat and a wool hat, smiling as he held snow in his gloveless hand. In the other, Adamu was laughing as he was sitting in the snow with the family dog standing nearby.

Under the pictures Christina wrote the date ŵhen they were taken and the words: "*Adamu's first snow*."

A bright, genuine smile quickly developed across his face as he enthusiastically said, "Wow. The cold snow. Ah! I can't believe it."

Smiling, Christina said, "Oh, turn the page, there is one more."

Adamu turned the page and saw a picture of him with Christina, William, and Nicholas all standing arm-in-arm in the living room at the pizza party following the 10K race.

"Nicholas took that one with his timer, remember?"

"Oh, yes. That was a great day! Thank you very much."

Just then William burst into the room, wearing a headband and an old Bradford College track team t-shirt that he found in the back of his closet.

"I am ready to run!" William shouted as he ran around the kitchen and pumped his arms, mimicking a runner in action. While he had lost some weight, he was clearly not yet in good enough shape to wear his old team t-shirt, which remained the size for a fit college athlete. He looked totally ridiculous—the short sleeves barely made it over his shoulders, and his mid-section poured out from the bottom of the shirt.

Christina and Adamu laughed loudly and Maggie barked at all the commotion.

"Hey, you laugh, but you're lucky I did not put this on," William said as he held up his old, incredibly tiny, track team running shorts over his head with both hands.

"Oh, my! Don't even think about putting it on," Christina shrieked in abject horror as the laughing and barking intensified.

William threw the shorts, along with a Bradford tank top, over to Adamu and said, "Adamu, you can have these. If I tried to put them on they would rip apart. I think they would fit you."

Coach Bellinger rode his trusted ten-speed bike over to Verona High. While waiting, he fiddled with the new stopwatch he had bought the day before. He was looking forward to seeing an old member of his team and to do a little coaching.

After the Volvo station wagon pulled into the vacant parking lot, a graying middle-aged man exited the car and excitedly said, "Hey, coach, how are you doing? Great to see you!"

As he shook Coach Bellinger's hand, William pulled in closer and the two hugged.

"Thanks for coming coach. It is wonderful to see you." Looking at the bike William said, "You're still riding your bike, huh? That's great."

William remembered how Coach Bellinger would ride his ten-speed bike around campus and alongside the team during training runs on the streets. The bike provided the coach with the opportunity to stay with his team on long runs and gave him a prime vantage point to provide instruction.

He had maintained the bike with care over the years, and it was still in good condition.

Being financially prudent, he never found the need to replace it. The old bike had earned its place as one of his most valued possessions.

"Yeah, it is great to see you too, William. Thanks for giving me a call to come down."

Turning to Adamu, William said, "Coach, this is Adamu."

As Adamu appeared from behind William, Coach Bellinger stepped forward and extended his hand to the meek and skinny-faced young man engulfed in clothes. The coach could barely feel Adamu's hand through the thick glove Adamu was wearing when they were shaking hands.

As they walked to the track, the coach told Adamu, "Don't try to do anything different or run harder than you normally do. Just a little running, okay? Nothing out of the ordinary. But before getting started we need to stretch and warm up."

Coach Bellinger sat down on the track and, with a hand gesture, invited Adamu to sit. Having never formally stretched before, Adamu found it to be rather odd, but he followed instructions.

Minutes into the various stretches, the coach looked up at William, who had been rambling on about what was happening in his life and said, "Hey, William, you can join us too, you know. I thought that you were running the marathon too."

William laughed and replied, "Oh, coach, not today. The last time you saw me running on a track, I ended up face down yelling in pain with a torn ACL. It would be embarrassing if you needed to call another ambulance for me, but this time for a pulled hamstring. Today, just Adamu is running. If you agree to help us with marathon training, you can put me to work later."

After the stretching, the coach continued to warm up Adamu by having him do some standing lunges, squats, jumping jacks, and a few short sprints.

As William looked on, he recalled how meticulous Coach Bellinger was in preparing his teams. While William was anxious to have Adamu run, he realized that, as always, Coach Bellinger was doing things the right way.

After the last set of jumping jacks, Adamu, who had broken into a sweat, took off his giant gloves, heavy jacket, and wool hat.

As the three walked over to the starting line at the mid-point of the track, Coach Bellinger said, "Adamu, I want to see you run a mile. Four laps around the track. Focus on running a nice even pace on each lap, okay? Okay, ready, go."

Coach Bellinger pressed the button to start the stopwatch and Adamu was off.

Studying Adamu's form as he tore around the track, Coach Bellinger yelled out, "Don't hunch over. Straighten up. Keep your chin up," as William anxiously looked over the coach's shoulder to try to sneak a look at the stopwatch. Unlike the previous occasions when he coyly kept William from knowing his true speed, Adamu was eager to show how fast he could run. He wanted to make a good showing for William and his old coach.

When Adamu finished the fourth and final lap, Coach Bellinger forcefully pressed the button on his stopwatch to stop the clock.

Greatly impressed, the coach exclaimed, "Great job, Adamu! Four minutes and fifty-three seconds" as he held up the stopwatch with a smile for William to see.

Adamu's talent was beyond what the coach had expected to see. Before he arrived, he figured he would just have Adamu run a mile, give him some pointers, and be done for the day, but he suddenly felt the charge of energy he used to get from coaching.

With his coaching juices flowing, he was compelled to evaluate Adamu's ability further with another test.

After giving Adamu a break to recover from his mile run, the coach said, "Okay Adamu. Now I want you to try a series of 200 meter runs. Take a minute break in between each run, but just keep going until I say stop."

While Adamu had an enthusiastic smile on his face, William felt a sense of dread in his stomach, for he had suffered through the same routine countless times when he was on the Bradford track team.

William emitted an uncontrolled audible groan, as he knew what his old coach was going to put Adamu through.

Coach Bellinger put the stopwatch away in his pocket as the next test had nothing to do with gauging Adamu's time—it was meant to assess his heart and determination. The coach had utilized the series of 200 meter runs over the years to see how long it would take a runner to feel fatigued and to see how they would react. Would he get discouraged and quit? Would he push harder?

As Adamu was off on his first 200 meter sprint, William said, in a plea for mercy, "Coach, I wanted you to look at him and to give him some pointers, not to run him into the ground."

The coach let out a smile as he recognized that William recalled the tough practices decades earlier.

"Just a little running, William. He will be alright. You were alright. You ate this up. You loved this stuff, remember?"

Coach Bellinger's comments were like a badge of honor being pinned on William's windbreaker.

Giving standout efforts in brutal practices was something William was known for at Bradford. The fact that his coach remembered his reputation decades later was very meaningful.

As a former pupil of the coach, William knew that the practice of having an athlete run multiple 200 meters in succession was not malicious; but rather, an important aspect of evaluation and training.

With each 200 meter sprint Adamu completed, Coach Bellinger looked closely for signs of him breaking down but, one sprint after another, he did not identify any appreciable signs of decline. While Adamu's pace understandably slowed, his form and positive attitude remained. He showed no signs of being a quitter.

"He might set a record for the most 200 meter runs without breaking," Coach Bellinger said as Adamu breezed through his fourteenth sprint with the same high intensity and resolve that he had exhibited in his first.

William swelled with pride, as he knew Adamu's strong effort in the 200 meter runs was far more remarkable than his fast one mile time. It showed that he had a fantastic level of determination, which even many gifted runners did not possess.

Excited by the prospect of coaching an incredible talent with a strong work ethic, and of reconnecting with a former member of his team, Coach Bellinger enthusiastically agreed to train William and Adamu for the marathon.

Mile 14

The next week, William and Adamu continued their running under Coach Bellinger's guidance. Because it was only the beginning of March, the coach said that the real training for the New York City Marathon, scheduled for the first week in November, could wait until early July.

Until then, he recommended that William run twelve to twenty miles per week to build a strong base. William was pleased that his "real training" could wait; he was swamped at work and felt he still needed to get his mileage up before beginning extensive marathon training.

The coach was so excited by Adamu's ability that he met with him four times a week. He relied upon the tried and true methods he had employed over the decades to instruct the first runner he had trained in years.

Riding his old bike alongside Adamu on the same scenic traffic-free roads he had his old teams use, the coach was back in the saddle, and he loved it. While the actual training for the marathon would not start for months, Coach Bellinger could not keep himself from challenging the gifted Adamu.

Of the hundreds of kids that he had coached over the years, Adamu had the most talent he ever saw. Besides his incredible speed, Adamu had great stamina and was quickly running seventy miles per week without a problem.

Frequently, Coach Bellinger, on his bike, would race Adamu at various points during long runs.

Besides being fun, he knew that the racing helped develop a runner's ability to run strong, even at the end of a run when they were fatigued.

Out on the roads Coach Bellinger would pick something out in the distance, such as a light post, and say, "Okay, Adamu, pick up the pace. Let's race to that post." When they were training on the high school track, he would often challenge Adamu to a one or two loop race.

Having the advantage on the bike, Coach Bellinger remained undefeated, but the races helped Adamu become a stronger runner.

Adamu, who never learned to ride a bike, would often try to ride Coach Bellinger's bike, but he never got too far.

"I think you need to stick to running. Next year you can try cycling," Coach Bellinger kiddingly told him after Adamu fell while trying to ride the bike.

Spending a large part of the week training with Coach Bellinger made Adamu wonder what his coach did when they were not together. The fact that his coach lived alone was sad and perplexing to him. In Sudan, the family unit was close and older people were an integral part of society. They were respected, imparted wisdom, taught values, and provided guidance to the youth regardless of whether or not they were related.

Adamu felt fortunate that he was able to spend time with Coach Bellinger and learn more about running from him.

When July finally rolled around, the coach provided Adamu and William with a comprehensive training plan that he thoughtfully constructed. He prepared two distinct ones, taking into account the skill level of his two runners, as well as, the time per week each could commit to training.

Both had to put in substantial miles, with a long run at the end of the week. Coach Bellinger, who was a proponent of including variety in a training program, devised each plan to include many activities such as speed work, hill work, plyometric drills, and weight training.

Due to his busy work schedule, William did most of his training during the week on his own. He got up early before work to run, and was also able to sneak in some mid-day exercises. The training was time consuming, but he knew he had taken his fair share of time off from being physically active over the past few decades. A few months of dedicated training was alright. He had pretty much reached rock bottom physically before he went running with Adamu in Duck Park the first time.

He had been cognizant of his decline for a long while, but always justified it away. He was always able to shift the topic in his mind and find a reason to continue his sedentary lifestyle.

But enough was enough.

When he initially reviewed the training plan prior to starting it, William felt overwhelmed—the weeks of training seemed endless, the steady mix of speed work, interval training, and weight work looked brutal, and the long run on the weekend looked like a dreadful way to end the week. But with each passing week, he felt himself getting stronger. He was dedicated to setting his alarm clock hours earlier than he had set it in years just so he could complete a training run.

It strengthened his resolve to know he was running when most people were snug in their beds.

Even adverse weather conditions did not stop him from keeping pace with his training schedule. Seeing people in their cars with looks of disbelief when they saw him running in the rain was like receiving an award. He gleefully labeled his dog a coward when she refused to follow him out the door to join him on a training run after she saw a driving rain outside.

His physical transformation matched the transformation of his mind as he continued to lose the fat that had found its place in his body over the years of inactivity. He wanted to fuel his body only with healthy food that would provide him with energy, so his diet improved. After weeks of healthy eating, he lost the desire to eat the bad food and snacks he used to indulge in.

Everything was coming together. Even his minute per mile pace was improving. Each week that he marked off his training log was like crossing a finish line. William was not so much transforming himself; rather, he was returning to who he was so many years earlier—a runner.

When he trained with Coach Bellinger and Adamu, the sessions made him feel like part of a team. They were working towards a goal together.

The camaraderie was special to him—it was just like the old days on the Bradford track team. The team dynamic helped him get through the months of training with a continually refreshed spirit.

Taking a break to talk with the coach during a training run at the high school track, William commented, "He is such a great talent," as he looked at Adamu running around the track.

"He is really something, William. He is without a doubt one of the most talented runners I have ever seen. And I have seen a lot of great ones. I feel for him, for what he has been through. He never talked to me about what happened in Sudan. He is a good-natured kid, but I can see that he is still hurting badly. It is really tough. I have read a lot about what is going on over there. Terrible. You know everyone is going to go through tough spots in life. I have. But what happened to him and his family is tragic. The loss of my wife was tough. It still is. But we had a good life. Except for not being able to have kids, we had everything we wanted and got to do pretty much everything we dreamed of. But he is still just a kid. And what happened there was just not right. He has a great work ethic on most days, but there are some times when he is just not there. The focus is not there. You can tell he is preoccupied and that his heart and his thoughts are somewhere else. And it is understandable. There are days when I see him running with tears in his eyes. When I see him like that, I pull back, wrap it up, and call it a day. It is tough to see him in pain. I think it is good for him to get out and train, especially for a goal like a marathon, but the pain is still definitely there."

Like William, Coach Bellinger also recognized that Adamu was struggling. He had come a long way in many respects but, while he was a warm and friendly person, the hurt and pain was still very much with him.

The coach continued, "It will take more time, but I think he is on the right path. He is a truly special talent. He has a bright future and can certainly do some great things in the running world. If he continues to develop, he can definitely compete at a high level and make some noise. But in order for him to be able to run to the best of his ability and fulfill his potential, he has to deal with his pain. Right now the pain is still holding his running back a bit. "

Coach Bellinger took a quick look at his stopwatch, shifted his eyes back up to study Adamu's form, and then added, "As a coach you have to get into each runner's head. You have to find out what buttons you need to push to help that specific runner reach their potential. Someone might need positive encouragement. Another might respond better to negative comments. You know how I was as a coach. With Adamu I clearly see that he still needs to deal with his past. At some point, he needs to address it. If he is able to do it, believe it or not, he will become a better runner. I also think that it will help him heal a little."

Coach Bellinger hollered instructions out to Adamu as he approached on the inside lane of the track: "Don't hunch over. Keep your head up. Don't swing your arms across your body like that. Work hard. Push it. Push it. Good Adamu. Way to work, great job."

When Adamu got closer he slowed his pace and motioned for William to join him.

Waving him on to continue, William said, "Next one. I'm still worn out."

Adamu smiled as he continued running on.

Mile 15

With the marathon approaching, Coach Bellinger began the process of tapering down the miles and intensity of the training for his two-man team so their bodies could recover and be in peak condition on marathon day. Both William and Adamu welcomed the tapering, but at the same time it made them anxious.

For Adamu's final practice, the coach put him through a light workout at the high school track while William was at work. As Adamu was approaching his final lap of a four mile run, Coach Bellinger grabbed his bike, which was leaning on a nearby fence.

He readied himself on it and shouted out, "Adamu, your last lap of marathon training is coming up—and your last chance to beat me!"

It was time for the final contest between Adamu and the coach. The race was on.

As Adamu approached on the inside lane, Coach Bellinger shifted his feet on the pedals and stomped down.

Because he was already in motion, Adamu flew by and was off to an early lead, but after a little over a quarter of a lap, the coach was on his heels. Since the coach was forced to take wide turns around the bends, Adamu would make his gains there, but then would lose ground to the coach on the straightaway.

The lead in the race went back and forth. Adamu usually had so much fun during the races with the coach, often having to try to keep himself from laughing, but on this day he was not in a laughing mood—he wanted to win.

Coach Bellinger also enjoyed the competitions, but he certainly was not going to give away any victories. Breathing heavily and sweating, the coach was aiming for an undefeated record.

Both competitors could tell this was the closest race they had throughout training. The anxiety level rose as they headed around the last bend of the track to the finish line. Coach Bellinger maintained a slight lead, but Adamu quickly recaptured the lead around the turn; then Coach Bellinger managed to catch up. It was a dead heat.

The question of who would win was going to be determined by who could beat whom in the last straightaway.

Adamu pushed hard and gave it all he had, while Coach Bellinger shifted gears and pedaled feverishly. Adamu took a slight lead, but the coach would not quit. With about twenty yards to the finish, Adamu could see the tire of the bike in his peripheral vision, and he could tell that the coach had inched into the lead.

Adamu ratcheted up his intensity and, with less than ten yards left, he retook the lead for good as his sneaker beat the tire to the line.

Adamu raised his arms in victory as Coach Bellinger slowed down his bike and looped back towards the finish line. Both were smiling.

Gracious in defeat and happy for Adamu, the coach said, "Great race, kid. You got me this time," as he dismounted from the bike and propped it against a fence. In between heavy breaths and holding onto the fence, he said, "Wow, you had a great finish. I was riding as hard as I could. You earned that."

Filled with confidence and determined to top his victory with one more, Adamu took hold of the bike. He swung his leg over the cross bar and sat on the seat.

He was ready to try to ride the bike again.

Catching onto Adamu's intentions the coach said, "Be careful, kiddo."

Undaunted and unafraid, Adamu positioned his feet, rotated the pedals, and propelled the bike forward. When the bike wobbled a bit, he balanced it and straightened the ride. The bike was still upright as a few more feet of progress was made.

As the bike crept forward, Adamu felt that he was close to claiming yet another triumph for the day as he was filled with an anxious confidence.

But then the bike drifted drastically to the right. His balance was lost. He tried to steady it, but he could not regain control as he veered towards a curb that surrounded the outside of the track. Smashing into the curb, the rim of the front tire bent in and collapsed. Adamu flew over the handlebars and crashed to the ground. The bike quickly followed and landed on top of him.

Coach Bellinger yelled out, "Adamu, are you okay?" as he ran over and pulled the bike off of him. "Are you okay?" he repeated.

Lying on the ground looking straight up, Adamu let out a groan and wearily said, "I am okay."

"Almost. You almost had it. You were so close to riding it," the coach said as he swatted debris off him.

When Adamu managed to sit up, he looked over at the damaged bike. Besides the damage to the rim of the front wheel, the handlebars were grotesquely bent, the seat hung from its post, and the light and reflector had broken off the handlebars and shattered into pieces. Adamu felt terrible. He had damaged something owned by someone who was so good to him. The good feelings from winning the race were gone. He started crying.

In between deep breaths he said, "I am sorry I damaged your bike" as his crying grew more intense. But the coach was not upset or angry in the slightest. He knew that the outpouring of Adamu's emotions was not totally a result of what just had happened. Damaging the bike was just enough of a trigger to open the floodgates of pain that was always with him, and the coach understood that.

He hugged Adamu tightly.

"Hey, it's nothing. Don't worry about it. This bike is older than you. It's okay, kid. And you are okay. You were so close to riding it too."

Laughing and patting Adamu on the chest, he added, "If the wheel wasn't so bent, you would probably do it on your next try," as he was able to coax a smile out of Adamu, and then a laugh.

Marathon training was over, but Adamu's bike riding would have to wait.

As they walked the bike to the coach's apartment, Adamu's spirits were restored as they exchanged stories about the months of training and talked about the upcoming marathon.

Between the time that they first met on the same track months earlier and the last day of training, Coach Bellinger helped turn Adamu from a raw talent into a trained, polished, and refined runner.

More importantly, two lonely and lost souls, who were both drifting in an ocean of pain, had formed a great friendship.

Adamu climbed out of the front seat of William's Volvo and moved to the back when Coach Bellinger approached the car. The coach settled into the front seat, closed the door, and pulled the seat belt across his body.

William shook the coach's hand and said, "Well, coach, thanks for letting us finally drag you out to dinner. Now that you helped mold us into lean, mean runners, let's load up on carbohydrates with some pasta. We are going to Renato's over in Ridgewood—the best Italian food around."

"Great, that sounds good to me. Thanks for taking me out. And you guys are going to do great in the marathon. You really are. When you come back from New York, it will be my turn to treat you guys, because I'll want to hear everything about it."

William pulled into the crowded parking lot of one of his favorite restaurants where he was a regular, and they made their way inside.

A busy hostess said, "Mr. Caldwell, as you can see, we are packed downstairs. Is it alright if we give you a table upstairs?"

"Yeah, that's fine, no problem."

"Okay, great, just head right up and you will be seated."

When the three made it to the landing at the top of the stairs, William and Adamu stepped back and let Coach Bellinger enter the room first, where twenty-five people shouting "surprise" welcomed him.

The room was decorated with maroon and grey streamers and balloons, the colors of Bradford College. A large sign that read *"Thanks Coach Bellinger"* hung on the wall. Coach Bellinger looked back at William and Adamu in shock. Both were smiling. They patted the coach on the back and gave him a slight push further into the room.

William held his hands up to quiet the room and said, "Coach Bellinger, in case you don't recognize these old folks, they are most of the 1974 Bradford College championship team. And in case you forgot, this year is the thirtieth anniversary of that championship which, as you know, was your first of many as a coach."

The room erupted in applause. "We wanted to get together to thank you. It was an exciting time. It was among the best times of our lives. And we have you to thank for that. You are a great coach and a great man, and we are all very lucky and fortunate to know you."

William passed a glass of soda to Adamu, handed a beer to Coach Bellinger, and then held his own beer. "So, we are all here to toast you. You're the best." The entire room joined in the toast and heartedly applauded again after everyone took a drink.

Christina came over and gave the coach a hug. "Hi, coach, good to see you again. Congratulations and thank you for everything—especially for getting William off the couch. I think he is even getting his abdominal muscles back."

"Thank you for all this. It's unbelievable. Thank you so much," the coach said as he looked around the room in disbelief.

Christina had suggested the idea for a party when William was trying to figure out what to get Coach Bellinger as a thank you gift for helping him and Adamu with the training.

When she realized it was the thirtieth anniversary of the coach's first championship team at Bradford, she suggested that they make the party even bigger by inviting the old team. In addition to the decorations, she also prepared homemade cookies, decorated to look like running shoes and Bradford tank tops, which she placed on each table.

Coach Bellinger enjoyed seeing his old team, and he surprised himself by remembering all of them and many of their accomplishments. Over dessert and coffee, John Cahill, the team captain, presented the coach with some gifts from the team—an engraved plaque commemorating the 1974 championship and two professionally framed black and white photographs.

One was a picture of the coach with the team after Bradford won the championship. The other was a photo of Coach Bellinger at a practice wearing a Bradford windbreaker—holding a stopwatch in one hand while a whistle hung around his neck.

As the party was winding down to an end, William stood up and said, "Coach, Adamu and I also wanted to thank you for all your time and efforts to help us with the marathon training. It has been great reconnecting with you. You have helped an old dog like me learn a few new tricks, and you have helped Adamu tremendously. You are a great friend to him. To thank you, we would like you to come with us to New York for the marathon. We have booked plane tickets and a hotel room for you. We hope you will accept."

The old coach waited for the applause of his adoring supporters to slowly fade. With liquid welling in each of his eyes, forming into tears that would soon journey down his wrinkled and worn face, he took hold of the back of an empty chair, breathed in deeply, exhaled slowly, and, knowing he faced the obstacle of trying to speak with emotion bundled up in his throat, he began to speak.

"Thank you, I would love to go. I always wanted to see New York. Thank you all. It means so much to me that you are all here and presented me with so many beautiful gifts. It's overwhelming."

The sadness of losing his wife flared up because he was thinking how he wished so deeply that she was there to share the moment with him.

"You know, we all talk about the good old days…I have had a lot of bad, lonely, and sad days over the last few years…so thank you, from the bottom of my heart, for reminding me of the good old days that we shared together…and for making today a day that, in the future, I will also consider to be one of the good old days."

As he dabbed the tears from his face with a handkerchief, the room yet again filled up with applause as he was enveloped in a sea of hugs.

As everyone began exchanging goodbyes, Christina whispered into William's ear, "One more thing, remember?"

"Oh right. Everyone, hold on. Hold on everyone. One more thing. Adamu wants to say something," William shouted over the clamor.

Adamu approached Coach Bellinger and, in a soft-spoken voice, began to address his friend and coach as the room quickly quieted down.

"Thank you for letting me be your student and for being my friend. You are a great man."

Adamu held up his hand to let everyone know that he was not done addressing the coach. He quickly walked over to the coatroom and disappeared into the small dark room.

After what may have been a moment too long, he finally reemerged with a bright and shiny present.

With a sheepish smile, Adamu navigated with care around the guests in his path and presented the gift, a brand new bicycle, to Coach Bellinger.

Adamu had outfitted the high-end road bike with a wicker basket and a horn on the handlebars. The wicker basket looked like something that he found in an antique shop, and the horn looked like something that a Marx Brother might have pulled from his jacket.

Neither the basket nor the horn would ever be found on a bike owned by a serious cyclist but, while somewhat out of place, they were great touches. They showed his innocence and generosity, as well as an intention to make the gift more special.

As she watched Adamu present the bike, tears of happiness cascaded from Christina's eyes, causing the makeup she had carefully applied hours earlier to stream down her face.

She realized that the gift exchange was an expression of love.

When Adamu showed up at the house with the new bike for Coach Bellinger the day before, she knew he once again had cut deep into his own savings to do something for someone else. But the purchase of the gift was touching enough of a gesture for her to decide to refrain from lecturing him about the importance of being conservative with his money.

"Thank you, Adamu. Thank you." Coach Bellinger could not speak anymore as emotion overtook him.

The coach and the pupil, two friends from different eras and different parts of the world, hugged each other tightly. The coach released his hug, but kept one arm around Adamu as he looked at the bike.

When he regained his composure, the coach said, "That's a beautiful bike. It sure is," as Adamu beamed with pride.

Then he asked, "Are you going to take it for a ride, Adamu?"

Adamu shook his head side to side in the negative and responded, "Uh, not tonight."

Coach Bellinger, William, and Christina broke into laughter. "Okay, not tonight," the coach said with a laugh. "We will have to wait until we get back from New York."

Mile 17

While the plane was in the process of making a turn to the right, the pilot announced that they were preparing to make the approach for landing at Newark Airport, just outside of Manhattan. After completing its turn, the plane was flying parallel with the entire island of Manhattan, providing Adamu with a great view as he looked out the window.

When he first arrived in the United States he landed in New York to change planes en route to Oregon, but it was a foggy morning and he did not see any part of the big city.

But now, as dusk fell, the lights throughout the city were illuminated, and he was treated to a spectacular first look at New York City.

Down below, the massive George Washington Bridge linking New Jersey and Manhattan spanned across the glistening Hudson River as dozens of cars and trucks darted across. Adamu spotted the little red light house at the base of the bridge on the Manhattan side and then took notice of the beauty of Riverside Church.

He was awed by the tall buildings of mid-town Manhattan, which looked like a great mountain chain. The impressive Empire State Building, dwarfing all the other buildings, was lit up in orange and blue, the colors of the New York City Marathon.

Sitting next to Adamu, Coach Bellinger leaned over to get a view and said, "There's New York City, Adamu. Amazing." Then he added, "If you can make it there, you can make it anywhere," referencing the lyrics in the song *"New York, New York"* sung by Frank Sinatra.

As they continued to Newark, the Hudson Bay came into view. "Hey, Adamu, there is the Statue of Liberty," Coach Bellinger exclaimed.

After a moment of searching, Adamu spotted it. Holding her torch up high, Lady Liberty looked tiny on a small island in the bay.

Like the thousands of immigrants who saw the statue when they arrived to their new country through Ellis Island over a century earlier, Adamu too was moved and inspired when he saw the famous symbol of freedom for the first time.

On the day before the marathon, Coach Bellinger, William, and Adamu decided to participate in a 4K run called the Friendship Run. The short course was used by many marathoners to keep limber before the big run, but more than anything else it is one of many fun events that bring people together on marathon weekend. The casual run began at the United Nations and ended at the finish line for the marathon in Central Park.

William was especially happy that Coach Bellinger decided to take part. While the coach was getting up in age, he was in great condition from biking and an occasional short run.

It seemed like the people of the world were coming together at the pre-race festivities near the United Nations as the smell of food and the sounds of music from numerous countries around the globe filled the air.

Thrilled, Adamu found tables where authentic African food was being served. He ate more than a fair share of his favorite dishes, which he had not tasted for well over a year, as he enjoyed African music being played by a large musical group.

Just before the start, he bought a Sudanese flag and a United States flag, both the size of a business card, from one of the many vendors.

The three-man team from Oregon leisurely completed the course by walking and jogging intermittently. After crossing the finish line, they congratulated each other, not so much for finishing, but for the role each had played in completing the training and for the friendship they shared. It was a fitting end to the marathon training.

The Jacob Javits Convention Center, a huge glass building with black tint located on 11th Avenue, is a fair distance from the heart of the city, but on marathon weekend the area seemed to be the epicenter of it all because it housed the Marathon Expo.

Adamu, William, and the coach fought through the crowd and made it inside, where William and Adamu were herded into an area where they officially checked-in and picked up their race packets.

The race packet included the race bib with the runner's number, a timing chip, and the highly coveted official marathon shirt.

While a huge variety of shirts and other accessories were sold at the expo, the official marathon shirt given to each runner was not for sale to the public. As long as the words "New York City Marathon" and the year of the race were printed on it, the official race shirt was always a close second to the finisher's medal as the most valuable memento a runner could collect on marathon weekend.

After they got their packets, and before heading over to meet up with Coach Bellinger, William excitedly rummaged through his bag so that he could get a look at the official marathon shirt.

Finding it, he pulled it out and held it up with two hands.

"Look at that, Adamu. We made it." Proudly looking at the shirt, which had a picture of a group of runners with the New York skyline in the background on it, he read aloud the words: "New York City Marathon." Adamu smiled as he watched William act like a little kid with a new toy.

When William tried to stuff the shirt back into the bag, a small plastic disc in a clear package fell out.

"Oh, I can't lose that, it's important," he said as he grabbed it off the carpet.

"What is that thing, William?"

"This little disc has a computer chip in it. All the runners attach it to their sneaker. During the race when they run over computerized mats located at different parts of the course, their times are recorded. Pretty amazing, huh?" Stuffing the disc back deep into the bag, William added, "It is also used to prevent someone from cheating in the race."

Music blared out over the loud speakers as they joined hundreds of others browsing the aisles where clothing and accessories were for sale. Numerous companies and running clubs set up elaborate displays for promotion, and many samples, such as sports drinks and energy bars were given out.

Stopping by all of the tables, Adamu, who was astounded that so many things could be related to the simple act of running, happily filled his bag with free samples.

When William spotted a table where he could register to run the marathon with a pace team, he eagerly signed up.

Pace teams, led by a seasoned marathoner who has the ability to run a certain pace throughout the entire race, are staples at most marathons. Participants who want to run a certain time often join a pace team to try to meet that goal.

William got in line to join a team seeking to run a four-hour marathon, which would require him to average at least a 9:09 minute mile throughout the race. While he was able to run a sub-9:00 minute mile pace in some distances in training, like a 10K and half-marathon, William often fell off that pace when running longer distances. Even though he knew that it was ambitious, and probably misguided, to attempt to finish the marathon in four hours he wanted to give it a try anyway.

Standing nearby, the coach cautioned William by reminding him that the rule of thumb was that a runner's marathon time would typically be no faster than that runner's half-marathon time multiplied by two plus ten to fifteen minutes. While he had run a few half-marathon distances in training in times of 1:58, 1:54, and a personal best of 1:51, it would be a challenge to meet his goal. Nevertheless, caught up in the excitement of the expo, and his hope for some "race day magic," he signed up to join the team.

He was given a chart that could be attached around his wrist, which displayed the time he would have to be at for each mile to meet his goal.

William responded to the coach's cautioned look with a big smile and a thumbs up.

"I can do it coach. I am a Bradford man, remember?"

With their bags full of free stuff, they turned down the last aisle and approached a table draped with a bright red banner and the word "Achilles" boldly written on it in white. A pioneer in the world of running warmly greeted them with a grin on his face and a glint in his eyes.

"Hi, I'm Dick Traum. Welcome to the expo. Let me tell you a little bit about us. My Achilles team is a running club for people with all types of disabilities who participate in events such as marathons."

Turning slightly to his right he said, "And these are two athletes that are a part of my team."

One athlete, a blind woman, was sitting in a chair with a black Labrador Retriever beside her.

The other athlete, a paraplegic, used his powerful arms to maneuver his wheelchair forward to greet them.

He extended his hand, "Hi. I am Nano, and this is Nooria."

Everyone exchanged handshakes and hellos, as Dick added, "Nooria and Nano are marathon regulars. They are competing again tomorrow."

Dick explained how Achilles was established, "In 1965 when I was twenty-four, I was hit by a car which resulted in my right leg being amputated. I went on to earn a Ph.D. and in 1970 I founded my own management consulting company. But, because of my amputation, I was not very active. So I found myself, at age thirty-four, grossly out of shape. After a friend my age had a heart attack, another acquaintance suggested that I join the YMCA. I had never really considered running or doing any type of exercise after my leg was amputated, but I joined and started to get active. Initially, it was a slow and grueling process, but eventually running ten minutes was possible. Soon after, a mile became easy. By May of 1976, almost eleven years after my accident, I completed my first race, a five miler in Central Park. It was so rewarding to be a part of a group and to accomplish something. It propelled me to do more and to dream bigger. Five months later, I became the first amputee to complete 26.2 miles when I ran the New York City Marathon."

"In 1983 we organized Achilles, a running club where one of our goals is to get people with disabilities involved in our sport. We have found running helps increase the comfort level of both the disabled population and their able-bodied peers. We help to raise the visibility of people with disabilities and seek to promote achievement. The achievement of completing a run for a person with a disability is addictive and each success increases expectations of what is possible."

Remembering the man he met at the 10K race he ran with William, Adamu said, "Mr. Traum, I met a blind runner at a race in Oregon. He was a member of Achilles."

"Yes, we have a great chapter in Oregon. We started Achilles chapters across the country, and we have chapters all over the world. We have thousands of members like Nooria and Nano who participate in many events, including marathons."

Adamu knelt on the floor and petted Nooria's docile dog. "I like your dog, Nooria. He is very good."

With a bright smile she said, "Yes, he is. His name is Yahoo. He is a loyal friend who helps me tremendously."

Despite losing her vision as an adult, Nooria Nodrat, relentlessly pursued her academic and athletic aspirations. Her determination and talents earned her a master's and doctorate degree, as well as, many marathon medals.

"Does Yahoo do the marathon with you too?"

"No. Yahoo takes a well-deserved break when I run. I complete the marathon with a guide. Are you going to do the marathon, Adamu?"

"Yes. This is my very first one."

"Oh, wow. That is so exciting. It is great."

Nano added, "Yeah, go for it in the marathon tomorrow Adamu. You will love it."

Like Nooria, being part of Achilles provided Nano Chilmon with a sense of belonging and accomplishment. He powered his sleek three wheeled handbike to the finish line in the hand cycle division in so many marathons that he had lost count.

He was intent on trying to set a personal marathon record the next day and finish the race within one hour and forty minutes. In an effort to inspire others, and to show his appreciation, Nano also serves as a coach for Achilles and frequently gives away the medals he earns to others.

William bought a copy of the book *"Go Achilles!"* that Dick Traum wrote which profiled many of the Achilles athletes. Dick told William the title was based on the phrase of encouragement that is shouted from the spectators at various runs when they see an Achilles member competing.

"Achilles athletes get big cheers at the marathon" Dick said. Then he added with a smile, "sometimes even bigger than the winners."

As the group exchanged their goodbyes and well wishes, Dick handed Adamu an Achilles patch and said, "Good luck tomorrow, Adamu. See you at the finish line."

Mile 18

After a few failed attempts, William finally hailed a taxi outside the Jacob Javits Center. The three slid into the backseat and were shuttled back to the Michelangelo Hotel on 51st Street.

At the hotel, Adamu poured all of the contents in the bag from the expo on his bed as William talked on the phone with Nicholas, who was about forty blocks south in his dorm room at New York University.

Bypassing most of the free stuff he received at the expo, Adamu picked up the "*Go Achilles!*" book and read with great interest about a woman from New York named Zoe Koplowitz, a marathon veteran who finished in last place in every marathon she completed.

Diagnosed with multiple sclerosis and diabetes, Zoe walks the entire route of the marathon on crutches. Taking anywhere between twenty-nine and thirty-three hours to complete the course, the Guardian Angels, a community safety group, accompany Zoe on her inspiring efforts which extend into the night and early morning.

Zoe was quoted in the book as saying, "It's not always about being first. It's about doing everything you do from the center of your being with all you've got. That's what makes you a winner."

Adamu then leafed through the official marathon program and read with pride about the impressive accomplishments of Onika Dura and Tafari Botha, two elite male runners from Africa, who were going to participate in the marathon with thousands of others the next day.

He turned the page and read a chart that included information about past New York City Marathons and was amazed to learn that only 127 people participated in the first one held in 1970, while 32,560 ran the race a year earlier. He then scanned a list of the recent male winners and their impressive finishing times of: 2:10.09, 2:09.14, and 2:08.45.

Adamu next became engrossed in an article about Grete Waitz, a nine-time New York City Marathon winner from Norway. He read how Grete, an accomplished 1500 and 3000 meter runner, never ran a marathon before participating in, and winning, the 1978 New York City Marathon.

Fred Lebow, the founder of the New York City Marathon, invited Grete to the marathon so that she could help set the pace for other runners. Although she did not have any aspirations to win, Grete's talent and strength helped lead her to a historic victory.

In 1992, long since retired, Grete accompanied Fred Lebow, who was suffering from brain cancer, in running the New York City Marathon. Grete stayed side by side with Fred as they ran and walked the entire course together; she said that the marathon she completed with the brave and courageous Fred was the most emotional race of her life.

Adamu was also impressed to learn that Grete went to the finish line the day after winning the marathon one year to cheer for Zoe Koplowitz of Achilles as she crossed the finish line.

William hung up the phone, clapped his hands eagerly, and announced, "Okay, Adamu, we have a plan. Let's go get the coach. We are going out for dinner. Then we are going to meet Nicholas in mid-town. He said he wants to take us somewhere as a surprise."

After enjoying a hearty meal at Sal Anthony's restaurant in the Little Italy section of the city, they were ready to top it off with dessert. While placing his order for a slice of ricotta cheesecake, William's cell phone rang out loudly. As he fumbled to find his phone, he received disapproving looks from a couple enjoying a romantic dinner nearby.

Seeing that it was Christina—who could not make the trip because of obligations with work—calling, he answered it while making his way outside. "Hi honey, I am in a restaurant right now; hold on while I go outside."

As William made his way out of the restaurant, Coach Bellinger talked to Adamu about the eventful day and the marathon, which was set to start in a mere thirteen hours or so.

"As we talked about in training Adamu, there will come a point in the marathon where you are really going to hurt physically and mentally. Expect it, don't be surprised or thrown off by it. You know in a lot of sports, it is good practice to visualize perfection going into an event. Golfers often think of the perfect swing over and over with the hope being that they will be able to replicate it in action. I think that long distance running is different. I think it's better to know going into a race that it's going to be a struggle. The pain and fatigue is inevitable, it will come. Maybe it will be at mile eighteen, mile twenty, mile twenty-two, but it will come. And when it does, that is the true start of a marathon. That is when you have to dig deep and grind it out. So, don't be shocked or demoralized when it comes. Embrace it. Embrace the pain. Use it as fuel. Say to the pain, what took you so long? Tell the pain, if you are here you better get on board because I am going to take you for a ride to the finish line."

From where he was sitting, the coach could see William outside through a window talking on his phone, and he watched him finish the phone call with Christina and then make a gesture to him that he would be a little longer.

When it appeared that William was waiting for another call to come in, Coach Bellinger determined that it was time to tell Adamu some things that had been on his mind for a long time.

"Adamu, I think it is appropriate that Dick Traum named his team Achilles. Achilles is a character in Greek mythology. As legend has it, when he was a baby it was known that Achilles was destined to be a great warrior. Fearing for his safety, his mother dipped Achilles in a river which had magical powers that would serve to protect him like a shield in battle. But when his mother dipped Achilles into the water she held onto him by the heel of his foot. So the protective water touched all parts of Achilles' body except his heel. Achilles became a great warrior and the magical waters helped to protect him. But one day, Achilles was shot with an arrow in the heel where the magical waters did not touch. As a result he died. Because of the myth, the term 'Achilles heel' has come to be known as an indication of vulnerability. I think 'Achilles' is a good name for Dick Traum's team because, while members of his team have a vulnerability, they still find the courage to participate and compete. "

He added, "The Achilles team reminds me of an ancient Chinese saying I learned a long time ago, *"Perseverance in weakness will lead to strength."*

The Coach looked out the window and saw that William was talking on his cell phone outside on the sidewalk, so he continued his talk with Adamu.

"Many runners have used their experiences as the reason to run and as the source of their inspiration. There was a great Ethiopian runner named Abebe Bikila who ran the marathon barefoot at the 1960 Rome Olympics and won. After the race, when asked why he ran barefoot, he said that he wanted the world to know that his country, Ethiopia, always won with determination and heroism."

"So, Adamu, it is okay to run with a mission, to run with something on your mind. It can be anger, it can be happiness—or something else, as long as it is focused. It can push you to do your best."

Sufficiently setting the foundation, Coach Bellinger was finally prepared to address his main point of the conversation.

"Now, Adamu, I know that you have been through a lot of loss and pain."

Adamu's head dropped immediately. His past was never really put out on the table for open discussion.

Coach Bellinger saw his reaction, but he felt that Adamu was strong enough to hear some things that he believed would help him if they were expressed.

"I know there have been times where your heart was not focused on training because you were thinking about your losses, and that is understandable. But, what I am trying to say is that I think it could be good for you to think about your pain when you are running. Confront it. It can be your inspiration. Because of what you have gone through, you will have the ability to attack the physical and mental pain that comes with long distance running in a way that is unique. It will make you a better runner. And more than anything else, I believe it will help you move forward in your life."

"Remember that ancient Chinese saying, *'Perseverance in weakness will lead to strength.'* Adamu, even though you may feel weak now, if you push forward in spite of it all, you will gain strength. I want to see you persevere, to push on, to make the most of your truly gifted talents and have the best life possible. You are the most talented runner that I have ever coached and you are a great person. I want nothing but the best for you. That is why I am telling you this."

Adamu understood the message that was being conveyed to him. He recognized that he was not the only one suffering from loss and that he needed to try to heal.

Adamu looked down at his hands, which were clasped together in his lap. Without looking up, he nodded to indicate he understood. He lifted his right hand and extended it across the table. Coach Bellinger took hold of it and held it tightly.

With the cell phone up to his ear, William walked close to the window of the restaurant and waved to Coach Bellinger. With hand gestures he asked the coach to send Adamu outside.

Without a jacket, Adamu shivered in the cold as he reached for the phone that William extended to him.

Hearing the voice of his own mother say his name through the tiny speaker on the phone was both as warming and shocking as it would have been if soothing rays of the sun suddenly appeared in the dark, frigid New York night and descended upon him.

Her voice and convincing words that it was true that she and his sister were alive and safe in a refugee camp in Ethiopia brought Adamu to his knees.

Moments earlier, Christina, shaking with excitement, could barely dial the phone to reach William on his cell phone when it was verified that Adamu's mother and sister had been located. Knowing that William was going to receive a call from the refugee camp in a matter of minutes, she was forced to keep her call brief, but it was the best phone call that she ever placed in her life.

When he completed the call and rose to his feet, Adamu felt reborn as a part of his empty soul was restored.

Mile 19

Filled with exhilaration from learning that his mother and sister were alive, Adamu's mind and heart were racing faster than the taxi he was sitting in, which was speeding through the city streets heading to mid-town. It then felt as if his body was matching his soaring spirit as he zoomed up seventy floors in the express elevator at 30 Rockefeller Center.

When the elevator stopped Nicholas led his father, Adamu, and Coach Bellinger out to the observatory deck to take in the magnificent sights. The illuminated metropolis below and the heavens above were on display in all their glory.

"I wanted to take you guys here because it is probably the best view of the city," Nicholas said as they faced south and viewed the Empire State Building, still lit in orange and blue in honor of the marathon.

"I also wanted to show you both the start and finish of the marathon."

Pointing to his left at a bridge lit up in the distance, Nicholas said, "Over there is the Verrazano Bridge. The right side of the bridge is Staten Island, where the race starts."

With his arm extended to show the direction, Nicholas explained how the runners would race over the Verrazano, into Brooklyn, and through Queens.

He walked to the side of the building and showed them the bridge over the East River that would take the runners to Manhattan, and then pointed out First Avenue, which the runner's would navigate as they ran north to the Bronx.

Then continuing to walk to the north side of the observation deck, Nicholas pointed at a huge dark rectangular shape, smack in the center of the city with just a few lights, and said, "And over there is Central Park. The finish line is near the bottom left portion."

While William enjoyed the view of the route he was going to traverse the next morning, seeing it was more intimidating than inspiring. "I wish you had showed me this *after* the marathon, not before it, Nicholas. That looks mighty far," he said with trepidation.

Adamu reflected as he looked out on the sprawling city below. From his high vantage point, the volume of the hustle and bustle on the streets below was muted.

He looked at the stars in the sky and saw the same constellations he recognized in Sudan, and he thought about home. His mother and sister were alive. The thought that they could see the same stars when the night fell in Africa brought him tremendous comfort; it made him feel that they were somehow closer. He thought about Tahir and Kirabo—who he never even saw smile—and hoped they could be as blessed as he was at this moment. It had been a long journey since that terrible night. He had endured a lot of pain and loss, but at this quiet moment he overflowed with appreciation.

Back at the hotel, Adamu and William arranged their things for the marathon. With cold weather expected early in the morning, William was glad he packed extra sweatshirts, sweatpants, hats, and gloves in preparation of the long wait before the start in Staten Island.

He even brought two sleeping bags he got on sale in preparation for the wait.

They planned to wake at 5:00 a.m., eat breakfast at the hotel, and walk a few blocks to where buses would take runners to the start. William had hoped to be in bed around 9:30 p.m., but due to the busy and exciting evening it was already 11:45 p.m., and he was still awake and getting anxious.

He hurriedly set out the shirt he was planning to wear in the marathon on the bed and taped two big pieces of masking tape about eight inches long across the front. With a thick black magic marker he wrote "William" in capital letters on the tape.

He had heard that when the spectators see the name of a runner on their shirts they would shout out personalized words of encouragement, which could provide an emotional lift he knew he was going to need at some point.

When the lights finally went off for the night, Adamu still had his eyes wide open, staring at the ceiling and deep in thought. It was one of the most momentous days of his young life.

His mind was racing as he thought about the miracle of having his mother and sister back in his life. He still had family—he felt alive again. He also thought about the stories of Abebe Bikila, the Achilles athletes, and Grete Waitz, and the words Coach Bellinger had said to him at the restaurant.

Adamu had found inspiration. He was ready to run.

Mile 20

When the ringing of the wake-up call was finally able to wake him, William instantly knew he had not gotten enough sleep. Groggy and unbalanced, he struggled to get out of bed and stand while fighting the urge to fall back into bed to sleep more. The soreness in his feet was proof that he had violated one of the rules that every marathoner should follow the day before the race—he did not stay off his feet enough.

Filled with regret, he was unsure if he was going to be able to give a good effort in the race that he had trained so hard for.

After a hasty breakfast, they hurried out of the hotel and walked a few blocks to a bus transporting runners to the start. Although they were bundled up, when they stepped outside at 5:45 a.m. onto the still dark and nearly desolate streets, the cold air chilled them to the bone. While the forecast called for clouds with temperatures in the mid-forties by mid-day, at the moment it was a harsh 29 degrees.

The bumpy ride, the excited talk of a group of first time marathoners sitting next to him, and the pungent smell of pain creams kept William, who was hoping to get a little sleep, awake for the entire bus ride.

When they got off the bus, they joined the herd of other runners on the long walk to the waiting area where already thousands of runners were waiting.

After they found a spot to set up camp, William rolled out his sleeping bag and crawled in. He adjusted a fleece headband, which was intended to protect his ears from the cold, over his eyes to block the light, and he twisted and turned in an effort to get comfortable. Exhausted, he was desperate to get some sleep.

After a little more than an hour, William was unsure if he actually slept. If he did it, it was not a deep sleep. He pulled the makeshift blindfold off his eyes, sat up, and looked around. While the area had seemed packed before, the number of runners around him had quadrupled since he had crawled into the sleeping bag. There was no space for anyone else to lay a blanket down.

The runners were everywhere.

While he initially thought he had found a prime spot to set up camp, somehow the area was turning into a major route for the thousands of others waiting for the start.

He looked to his right. Adamu's sleeping bag and bag of clothes remained untouched.

Deciding he better load up on some of the free food and drink available, William climbed out of his sleeping bag. When he took a deep breath and exhaled with exasperation, the cold in the air made his breath visible like a smoke-blowing dragon.

Despite the cold, the long lines, the extensive wait, and his tiredness, he was thrilled and excited to be there. He was in New York and was going to run in the New York City Marathon. He could not believe it. After all the years away from running, he was about to participate in the biggest marathon in the world.

While struggling to carry two bagels, a banana, a bottle of water, and a coffee back to his campsite, William fought his way around the multitude of runners occupying Staten Island. Many luxurious little camps peppered the area—some had comfortable chairs, others had tents, and some even had inflatable mattresses. It was a festive atmosphere.

William was astonished to see that some runners were apparently planning to wear costumes while running. One person was dressed in an ape suit, another was wearing a light blue tuxedo with a ruffled shirt and cummerbund, and someone else was wearing a superhero costume.

Like the wave of immigrants that came to New York through nearby Ellis Island over a hundred years earlier, many of the runners came from distant countries to participate. He spotted a group of runners from a running club from Italy, and then another from France, and yet another from Mexico. Some wore the flags of their countries on their shirts and some painted them on their faces. It was truly an international event.

When William made it back to his modest little campsite, Adamu's bag of personal items and rolled up sleeping bag still remained untouched, and Adamu was nowhere in sight. Even though it was nearly two hours before the start, William began getting a bit worried about not seeing Adamu for so long. As he ripped off a piece of his bagel, he finally spotted him off in the distance warming up, as he vigorously went through a quick succession of the routines that they had performed numerous times in training.

William watched with wonder for nearly forty-five minutes as Adamu intensely ripped through set after set of exercises and stretches.

When Adamu finally returned he was sweating profusely.

"Looking good, Adamu," William said as he handed him a bottle of water and bagel. "You might be overdoing it a bit. We still have nearly an hour before our start. Relax. The elite men are just getting ready to start soon."

"Really? I want to get close to the start to see it."

"Adamu, there are too many people. We can never get close. Besides, we probably won't be able to see anything."

"Oh, but I really want to try. I want to see some of the African runners up close."

Not wanting to diffuse Adamu's excitement, William said, "Okay, you can give it a try. I am going to meet up with my pace team soon anyway. Good luck, kid. You are going to do great. Have fun."

"Okay." Then Adamu asked, "Is it okay if I wear your stopwatch for the race?"

William was slightly thrown off by the request. Adamu never cared about his time before, and William actually wanted to wear his watch to gauge his own time during the run.

Nevertheless, he said, "Yeah, sure. I don't really need it. I am going to be with my pace team anyway."

As William worked to get the watch off his wrist, Adamu started the process of taking off the many layers of the clothes he was wearing. When Adamu was down to an old pullover and sweats, William figured that Adamu, who was always bundled up in the cold, was not going to take any more clothes off.

But to William's surprise, Adamu then peeled off his sweatshirt and sweatpants and was left wearing nothing but a tank top and shorts. Without wearing his usual concealing clothing, Adamu looked like a finely tuned athlete as perspiration floated off his body into a heavy mist.

Although he always appeared to be almost too skinny, lean muscles exploded all over Adamu's body and raised veins zigzagged up and down his arms and legs.

But William's heart sank when he finally became aware of the reason why he never saw Adamu wear a tank top or shorts before.

A massive scar from the upper portion of Adamu's back extended to his right deltoid and then worked its way down his arm nearly to his elbow. Another huge scar was visible on Adamu's left shoulder and upper chest.

Discolored and raised, the scarring was severe. Similar scarring was also noticeable on the middle of Adamu's left thigh. The scar on this thigh, which had a deep impression with scarring that surrounded the circumference, looked like a volcanic crater.

It was clear the scars were from the attack.

The scar from the surgery performed by Dr. Zamora was also visible as it extended from just below his left knee mid-way to his ankle.

Inspired from his experiences the day earlier, Adamu decided that the time had come to uncover his physical scars and to confront his emotional pain.

William was also taken aback at what Adamu was wearing—his old Bradford tank top and shorts—the ones that he tossed to him in the kitchen on the morning that they were going to meet with Coach Bellinger for the first time.

Although faded, the word "Bradford" was still visible on the front of the tank top and on the right side of the shorts.

Adamu used safety pins to attach the small United States and Sudanese flags, and the Achilles patch, which he got the day before, on the tank top just above where "Bradford" was printed.

Deciding to focus on what Adamu was wearing, and not the scars that covered his body, William excitedly said, "Hey, you got the old Bradford gear on! Look at that. That is great! Really awesome, Adamu. Really cool."

"I wanted to represent you and the coach—my team—in the run."

Touched by Adamu's words and gesture and saddened by the scars, William instantly felt a lump develop in his throat. He pulled Adamu in for a tight hug and said, "That's right, Adamu, we are a team. Thank you. Thank you, Adamu. Good luck. Run a great race. You trained hard. Go get it out there."

After William released his embrace, he handed over his stopwatch and Adamu darted away, disappearing amongst the throng of runners already lining up for the start.

A short time later, over a loud speaker, Allison Millman, the head of the New York City Marathon, introduced and gave a brief summary of the impressive career accomplishments of each of the elite male runners before they would be given a separate start in front of the main field of approximately 38,000 runners. Standing about thirty yards away from the start line, Adamu listened and clapped after each runner was introduced.

The mayor of New York City bellowed over the speakers on the sound system: "On your mark, get set," and then a loud horn sounded. Then the elite runners were off as the song *"New York, New York"* filled the air.

Adamu laughed when he recognized the lyrics in the song *"if I can make it there, I can make it anywhere,"* as the phrase that Coach Bellinger had been repeating over and over since they arrived in New York. Just the day before the coach had explained to him what the phrase meant when he asked about it.

While he waited for his start, Adamu was focused, inspired, and determined. Just like what Frank Sinatra sang, he was ready to try to make it in New York.

Mile 21

Earlier that same morning Nicholas left his dorm room and met Coach Bellinger at his hotel. For a young college kid who rarely missed going out on the town on a Saturday night, it was by far the earliest that he had ever woken up on a Sunday while at NYU. They caught the number 6 subway to the 138th Street station in the Bronx, which was just a short distance from the mile 20 marker on the marathon course.

Nicholas learned from a friend that the area near mile 20 was a great spot to watch the race, because it was far less crowded than most parts of the course and, as such, it gave the spectators a better chance to see the person they wanted to cheer on.

Also, because mile 20 was part of the run where a runner would likely feel depleted and "hit the wall," it was a perfect place for Nicholas and the coach to give Adamu and William some needed support.

Leafing through the marathon program he picked up at the expo, Coach Bellinger took notice of a chart which gave spectators an idea of when they could anticipate seeing a runner at different points in the race based on their expected pace.

While he hoped William could meet his goal of a 9:09 minute mile, he figured that it was more likely that William would run no faster than a 10:00 minute mile. While he knew Adamu was incredibly fast, he figured that Adamu would probably be slowed by the crowded course and distracted by the sights and sounds along the way. The chart suggested that Adamu and William would not reach mile 20 for at least a few hours. Settling in for a long wait, the coach and Nicholas held their coffees with both hands for warmth in between bites of bagels and donuts.

After struggling to get through the congestion of the other runners lined up for the start, William got within about twenty feet of his pace team.

It was impossible for him to actually figure out who was part of the team because the crowd of runners was so thick. The pace team guide was holding a stick with a sign which said "4:00" that extended high in the air for members of the team to see. Bright orange and blue balloons were attached to the sign to help team members keep track of the pace leader.

William and the other runners stood still waiting for nearly fifteen minutes. Then, like a train car part of a long line of cars, the group of runners were slowly, but suddenly, headed to the start en masse. While a collective sound made up of a mix of claps and excited utterances filtered throughout, William remained quiet. Fear and anticipation ran through his mind as he realized he was really about to try to run 26.2 miles—a distance he never ran before. Although he was consumed with the marathon for months, the first few steps towards the start were a scary reality.

The walk to the starting line lasted nearly fifteen minutes. Along the way runners began to peel off the layers of extra clothes they wore to stay warm and dropped them on the ground. William had to step over piles of discarded sweat pants and sweatshirts which, after all the runners left Staten Island, an army of volunteers were prepared to retrieve and provide to the needy.

As he struggled mightily to get his sweat pants off, especially over his sneakers, the runners walking from behind bumped into him, and the leader of his pace team had advanced about fifty feet ahead.

Filled with anxiety, he could not help but feel that he was lagging behind before he even crossed the starting line.

Because of the huge amount of runners, there would not be an official starting horn for William and the others near him before they crossed the starting line to officially begin their run. The start line was a big mat with a computer device which, in conjunction with the computer chip on his sneaker, would record that he started the race.

As he crossed over the starting line, William felt like he had just jumped out of a plane to sky dive. He thought to himself, *"This is really happening…no turning back now."*

Although he was still filled with a heavy touch of anxiety, the scene and mood as the runners started their one mile trek over the Verrazano Bridge into Brooklyn was like a carnival. Boats from the New York City Fire Department in the bay below shot water up in the air like giant fountains to celebrate the start.

Many runners were joking and laughing; some stood on the side and took pictures of each other and of lower Manhattan which could be seen from the left side of the bridge. Many lined up next to a speed limit sign on the bridge for a unique photo.

As he charged across the bridge, which was the biggest incline on the course, it seemed as if the massive structure was moving from side to side and up and down.

Hoping he would not get dizzy, William kept his eyes focused on the balloons of his pace leader and fought his way back closer to his team. When he was within twenty feet or so, he relaxed a bit and determined that he was close enough. He reasoned that it was not worth the effort to get closer as long as the balloons remained in sight.

When the course led him into Brooklyn, William was absolutely overwhelmed with his first taste of the New York spectators. People were everywhere—they were lined four rows deep on the sidewalks, they were on fire escapes, and they were leaning out from windows. Cow bells were ringing, noise makers were operating, and hands were clapping. Inspirational music blasted out from different places. Words of encouragement were displayed on signs and shouted out. One sign stated, *"You are not a runner, you are a Marathoner,"* another read *"Why 26.2 miles? Because 26.3 would be crazy,"* while yet another read, *"I know a shortcut."*

William was told that the spectators were supportive at the marathon, but he was skeptical. He figured that tough, jaded New Yorkers would not be as supportive as people said. But he was happily proven wrong. The support was absolutely unbelievable.

The route turned down Fourth Avenue and he took in the incredible sight of thousands of runners ahead of him on the wide avenue that extended straight for miles. Like waves in a flowing river, the tightly packed runners bobbed and swayed as they ran. The different colors of their clothes blanketed the avenue like confetti. Not an inch of the dark road could be seen. Each speck of color had the same goal—to cross the finish line in Central Park. Inspired to be one of those specks, William felt he could practically sprint all the way to the finish line about twenty-five miles away.

Adamu, on the other hand, did not get to see the same glorious sight about fifty minutes earlier when he turned onto Fourth Avenue. While lined with spectators, the broad roadway was practically empty. Just a few scattered runners were in his vicinity, while, further down the road, a small group of the elite men were gracefully churning out a torrid pace as they headed towards Queens.

Adamu, and the other runners near him, were off to a fast start; however, with about twenty-five miles to the finish line, the race, in effect, did not start. Adamu was not, and would not be, the only runner off to a blistering fast start in the marathon.

Adamu tried his best to heed Coach Bellinger's advice to keep a nice comfortable pace in the early miles to conserve energy, but it was difficult to temper his excitement.

Hours later, the lead pack of elite men dwindled to three runners just past the twenty-three mile mark: defending champion, Onika Dura of Kenya, Tafari Botha of Nigeria, and Jose Silva of Argentina. The year before Dura bested Botha by a mere three seconds in one of the closest finishes ever, and two years earlier Botha beat second place finisher Dura by twelve seconds.

On this day yet another chapter in the bitter Dura and Botha rivalry was being written.

Onika Dura's aggressive attitude, on and off the racecourse, helped fuel the rivalry with Tafari Botha. Dura was a very serious and tough runner who tried to intimidate his competition with a stare or a carefully placed elbow when a run got too congested.

He made it a point not to fraternize with the other runners—he did not even congratulate Botha on winning the New York City Marathon two years earlier. Dura actually went so far as turning his back on him when Botha offered him congratulations for a good effort.

In contrast, Tafari Botha was very affable and had a great reputation with the other runners, including Jose Silva, the other runner in the group running hard to complete the last three miles of the course. In fact, over the years Botha and Silva ran practice runs together and exchanged advice.

The bond between Botha and Silva certainly gave them an advantage over Dura in the final stretch of the race. Botha and Silva each wanted to win, but certainly would rather have the other win instead of Dura. However, despite Botha and Silva's coordinated efforts to try to deplete Dura's energy down the home stretch, Silva fell off the pace just past the twenty-five mile mark and Botha fell behind Dura with about a quarter mile to go.

Onika Dura crossed the finish line with the winning time of 2:08:12.

Earlier when the pack of lead male runners crossed the Willis Avenue Bridge connecting Manhattan to the Bronx and ran past Coach Bellinger and Nicholas, the coach figured that, because the general field had started after the elite male runners, it would take some time before a runner from the general field would pass. But very shortly after the elite men ran by, the coach was surprised to see a lone runner, who he would find out was a runner from the general field, charging across the bridge.

"This guy is flying," Coach Bellinger said out loud to no one in particular.

As the runner got closer, the coach grabbed Nicholas and said, "I don't believe it. It is Adamu."

Caught off guard because he too did not expect to see Adamu so soon, Nicholas rushed to put his coffee down as he shouted, "Yeah, Adamu. Go, Adamu, go!"

Besides seeing Adamu running for the first time in shorts and a tank top, Coach Bellinger saw an intense determination he had not seen before in his pupil. But the coach certainly recognized the look.

He knew that Adamu was mentally in the place that he had held off on trying to push him to in training. He knew Adamu was embracing his pain and was using it to reach a level of optimum performance. The coach could tell that Adamu had added the strength of will to his great talent.

Despite Nicholas' loud screams, Adamu did not hear anything and did not see Nicholas or his coach. Adamu's speed and focus left them in awe.

After Adamu flew by, Nicholas said, "He was ripping."

"Yeah, he was ripping alright," Coach Bellinger said as he looked at his watch and tried somehow to figure out the pace that Adamu was running. He realized he was not going to be able to figure it out because he wasn't sure when Adamu had actually started. But, based on the short amount of time that elapsed between the moment the elite male runners and Adamu crossed over the Willis Avenue Bridge, he was able to make an educated guess that was hard to believe.

"Adamu just might win this thing," he said in amazement to Nicholas as he tried his best to quickly explain the basis of his belief. Then he said, "I'm sorry Nicholas, but I have to get to the finish line."

Nicholas grinned, "Okay, I will take you there."

"No, it's okay, stay. Your dad expects to see you here. He will likely be struggling when he gets here and when he sees you it will lift his spirits. If you are not here it could really bring him down. Just tell me what subway to take. I will find my way."

Nicholas gave the coach a quick lesson on how to navigate the subway. Confident that the coach could get to Central Park safely, Nicholas handed him his Metro Card to pay for the ride and, with a smile, told him that he would meet him at the finish line later.

Mile 22

"Welcome to mile 8 runners!" the man on the platform screamed into the microphone as William entered a part of Brooklyn with beautiful brownstone houses lining a narrow street. Running through a wall of sound created by a high school band triumphantly playing the inspirational theme from the movie *Rocky,* it felt as if all of the cheers from the spectators, who flowed onto the street, were for him.

Later, when he and his pace team were almost across the lower deck of the quiet, dark, and spectator-free 59th Street Bridge linking Queens to Manhattan, William could hear the raucous crowd awaiting the runners in Manhattan.

With each stride forward, the unseen crowd got louder and louder. With the sun suddenly breaking through the clouds and dramatically shining into the lower deck of the bridge, William brimmed with anticipation as the decibels of the cheers increased. When he finally reached the end of the bridge and set foot onto the island of Manhattan, he pumped his right fist in the air with excitement to the spectators packing the sidewalks.

With about ten more miles to the finish, he took inventory of his condition and concluded that everything was going perfectly. No pain anywhere and he was keeping up with his pace team without any problem. In fact, he felt the group was holding him back. Buoyed by the support of the spectators, he picked up his pace.

He was filled with confidence as he left his pace group behind and charged north on First Avenue.

Although he had been running by himself for miles, beginning in the middle of mile 23, Adamu had company. Twinges of physical pain and mental fatigue were making more frequent visits to his body and mind and the unwelcomed visitors felt like they were asking him to slow his pace.

The route of the course took a right turn and led Adamu off of Fifth Avenue and onto East Drive in Central Park. Along the roadside, he noticed one of the large rocks part of the landscape.

From a certain angle, the rock resembled the shape of Lafon Hill in Sudan, which he raced to with his friends, and he instantly felt a jolt of energy from the memory of the time he and his friends shared at the top.

While fully aware he was running in the largest urban settlement in the United States, in his mind it was Sudan, and he was running side by side with Naeem, Salim, and Dukarai.

As he looked ahead down the road, he did not see the buildings—he saw the mountains of Sudan. He did not see the street lights in the distance—he saw the long necks of the camels that walked the land. He did not see spectators lining the course—he saw the tall grass near his village waving in the wind. He did not hear the cheers from the spectators, but instead heard the voice of Salim shouting out the same words of encouragement he yelled on the day they were sprinting to Lafon Hill—*"Go, Adamu, go!"*

After he passed the mile 24 marker, he turned his left wrist and took a quick look at the watch he borrowed from William. From the moment he pressed a button on the old Timex when he crossed the starting line, the device had been keeping track of the time of his effort to the millisecond.

Without skipping a stride, he calculated his pace, considered the distance to the finish line, and concluded he had the opportunity to meet his goal.

Adamu was intent on having the fastest time in the race.

Like the great Grete Waitz, he was determined to make history in his first marathon and win the New York City Marathon.

While lying in bed the night before, Adamu's mind raced as he recounted the developments of the day: the miracle of learning that his mother and sister were alive, the words Coach Bellinger said to him at the restaurant, and the inspirational stories of the Achilles team, Abebe Bikila, and Grete Waitz. Reading about the history of the marathon and learning about the incredible and inspiring feats of different marathoners, Adamu was grateful to be part of such an event. He recognized how running could give so many people hope and provide them with a sense of accomplishment.

He realized that, although he had lost a lot, he still had plenty to be thankful for. He decided his marathon effort was going to be a dedication to what he lost and a celebration of what he still had.

After reading the list of recent winning times in the marathon guide, Adamu determined he was capable of matching those times. Recalling what William told him about the timing device on his shoe, he realized nothing was stopping him from trying to be the fastest runner in the race.

While he recognized that, during the race, he would have no way of knowing what time would be needed to have the fastest time of the day, he knew that, if he could get close to equaling the time of the recent winners, he had a chance to meet his goal.

But the pain and fatigue would not relent.

The lofty goal he had set for himself felt like it was slipping away. He was weakening.

For some reason the mythical story of Achilles entered his thoughts and somehow, instead of thinking about Achilles being dipped into the water by his mother, the image of Tahir dipping him into the river in Sudan flashed through his mind.

It had been the lowest point in his life. He remembered how vulnerable and weak he was at that moment.

But then he recalled how Coach Bellinger once told him to dismiss any negative thoughts when the physical and emotional strain of the marathon built up. *"Turn all negative thoughts into positive thoughts that can help get you through,"* the old coach had said.

So Adamu did. He thought about how, unlike Achilles' mother who did not fully dip Achilles in the magical water that protected him, Tahir did completely submerge him under the water that terrible night.

Adamu's recollection and the comparison with Achilles allowed him to convince himself that, unlike Achilles, he was invincible—at least for the remaining miles of his quest to be the fastest runner in the race.

He felt that nothing could prevent him from achieving his goal.

He continued to think about his personal journey, his losses, his pain, and the suffering and deaths he witnessed. In the past when he thought of such things, there was a swelling of pain in his stomach that spread throughout his body, which served to cripple his drive and stymie any aspiration of hope.

Now his thoughts created a swelling of purpose and drive from deep inside his soul, which strengthened his heart and resolve.

His perseverance had led to him to find strength.

Inspired by the thoughts in his mind, carried by the determination in his heart, and propelled by the talent in his legs, Adamu increased his pace despite the pain and his dwindling energy reserves. He pushed towards the finish line with such a frantic, yet controlled, urgency it was almost as if he thought that, if he did not complete the race as fast as he could, the finish line would, like a sun setting on the Sudan horizon, disappear before he could reach it.

Accomplishing his goal to be the fastest runner of the day would allow him, for a moment, to be like a boy again, not a Lost Boy, but a boy, when all in his life was innocent and beautiful. Focused on the road ahead, he ran the last two miles of the marathon like he was running up Lafon Hill.

He ran with the spirit of a boy pretending to be a lion.

Mile 23

Scanning the clothes and faces of thousands of runners, hour after hour, trying to spot his father was a dizzying task. When he finally saw his father, who was trudging along so slowly that it barely qualified as running, Nicholas shouted out, "Yeah, Dad! Go, Dad!"

William's decision to run ahead of his pace team proved to be a costly mistake. After a fast-paced mile, he began to struggle and slow down. When his team caught back up to him he tried his best to stay with the group, but the damage had already been done.

Unable to maintain the pace that was easy for sixteen miles, he fell behind and dejectedly watched the balloons that his pace guide was holding disappear from his view.

While the vision of runners bobbing up and down ahead of him along Fourth Avenue in Brooklyn inspired him hours earlier, the same type of sight along First Avenue had made him woozy.

With a tough 6.2 miles remaining, a stretch most say is the most difficult part, he was hurting all over. His hamstrings were tight, his legs were heavy, his feet ached, he had a rash from his shorts rubbing his skin, and even his forearms were stiff from holding his arms in the runner's position.

But most of all, he was hampered by an intense pain on the side of both knees which developed in the midst of his ambitious and ill-advised charge up First Avenue.

With each slow stride he was able to grind out, the pain shot through the side of his knees like a lightning bolt.

The knee pain was particularly severe whenever he was forced to turn or run on anything but a flat surface. With the high amount of turns in the route and depressions in the streets, the course itself, in addition to the distance, proved to be a challenge.

Running with the grace of a shopping cart with a broken wheel, the proper form William had hoped to maintain was lost somewhere on First Avenue and 68th Street.

He was in the midst of a mental battle where he was trying to will himself to the finish. While he knew he already had fallen well behind his goal pace, he was fighting to give a strong effort in spite of the adverse circumstances.

He was gutting it out.

While happy to hear the voice of his son shouting encouragement, he felt a sense of dread when he saw Nicholas on the far side of the street, for he knew that his knees would ring out in pain when he attempted to run on a sharp angle across the street through the wave of other runners to be able to get close to him.

"Looking good, Dad. Looking good," Nicholas said, in spite of the overwhelming visual evidence to the contrary, as he suddenly felt guilty about challenging his father to run the marathon.

Fearing that if he came to a complete stop to talk the pain and fatigue would not allow him to start running again, William motioned to Nicholas to move down the road with him as they chatted.

With Nicholas able to keep pace with just a fairly slow jog, William said, "Hey, son, I'm struggling. My knees are in bad shape. I was feeling good so I ran ahead of my pace team. Then I ran out of gas and my team caught up and passed me by. I am in survival mode now."

William was also being tested by the elements. Although it was cold in the morning, by the time he reached First Avenue, the sun had come out and the temperature rose a great deal which helped to sap his energy even more. In the midst of his struggles he half-jokingly thought how the elite runners had it easy, for they were finished in just over two hours while he and the other mortals had to be out on the course much longer.

"Let me tell you, it is tough when someone running in a banana costume followed by another person in a gorilla costume passes you by," he said with a self-deprecating laugh. "Hey, where is the coach? Did you see Adamu?"

As he jogged alongside his dad, Nicholas said, "When Adamu passed he was flying, I mean *really* flying. He was all by himself. No one was close. And he looked real serious; he did not even talk or wave. Coach headed to the finish line. He said that Adamu passed this point a lot sooner than he expected. He thought that Adamu actually had a chance to win the whole marathon."

"What?" William asked, as the information was enough of a shock to bring him to a stop.

"Yeah, that's what he said."

William tried to digest what he had just heard. "Wow, that's crazy, I better get going. See you at the finish line, kiddo."

With a quick hug and more encouraging words from his son, William tried his best to resume his run while trying to comprehend what he was just told.

He first thought there was no way Adamu could actually win. But then he thought about how Adamu did have an amazing gift and how the coach seemed to be right about these things. He thought about how Adamu had vigorously warmed up before the start and how he had asked to borrow his stopwatch even though he was never interested in his time before. He also remembered how Adamu was running in a tank top and shorts—in the cold no less.

As he gingerly shuffled through the Bronx, William thought that maybe, just maybe, it was possible that Adamu could win the New York City Marathon.

Because the elite male and female runners had already finished, the officials for the New York City Marathon felt more relaxed and at ease in the large tent situated to the right of the finish line.

Second and third place finishers Tafari Botha and Jose Silva were enjoying hot tea and food together while Onika Dura, the top male finisher, lounged on a chair alone, but basking in victory nonetheless.

After chatting with the female winner, Ginette Bedard of France, Alison Millman, the head New York City Marathon official, announced that the presentation of the awards would take place in twenty minutes, just outside the tent at the winner's podium.

Far off in the corner of the tent closest to the finish line, Jason Schmidt, an intern for the New York City Marathon, sat at a desk in front of a television and computer. The television showed a live feed of the finish line from three separate angles. Wires ran from the computer under the tent to the mat at the finish line.

As each runner crossed the mat, his or her time would be logged in the computer in order of the fastest to the slowest finisher.

While holding a donut in one hand and a cup of coffee in the other, Jason looked at the computer and the television feed to ensure that everything was still working properly.

On the television screen he saw a lone runner wearing a maroon tank top with grey trim approach the finish line. Jason glanced at the computer and looked at the column on the screen that kept track of the number of runners who completed the race. As expected, he saw the number increase by one when the runner crossed the finish line. However, he also heard the sound of a bell emanating from the speakers of the computer, so he moved closer to the computer screen to try to determine what caused the bell sound to ring out.

Looking at the list of the finishers, he saw that the name and the finishing time of a runner on top of the list was highlighted. The highlighted name was Adamu Jabari, and his finishing time was 2:08:07. The name Onika Dura with a time of 2:08:12 was *below* Adamu's name. With an audible gasp, Jason looked at the names and their corresponding times again.

The number "*1*" was next to Adamu's name and the number "2" was next to Onika Dura's name.

Jason quickly shifted his eyes over to the live television feed. The runner with the maroon tank top who had just crossed the finish line was hunched over catching his breath. Then he stood up straight and walked out of the picture frame. Scrambling to get out of his seat, Jason dropped his donut and spilled his coffee.

Running out of the official's tent he yelled, "Hey, someone stop that guy."

Somehow, someway, Coach Bellinger made it to Central Park before Adamu and got himself a spot near the finish line where he was able to see the talented runner he trained complete the race.

As he watched Adamu charging towards the finish line he looked as strong, if not stronger, than he did when he crossed over the Willis Avenue Bridge near mile 20. Coach Bellinger's heart pumped with excitement as Adamu pushed towards the finish line with grit and determination.

The coach himself lunged forward when Adamu was about to cross.

After crossing the finish line, Adamu, who had just gracefully ran 26.2 miles with perfect form, took a few clumsy steps and slowed to a stop. Breathing heavily, he bent over and put his hands to his knees, which almost buckled.

Driven past his physical and emotional limits, he took deep breaths and walked a few steps to where a volunteer, with excited words of congratulations, placed the finisher's prize, a copper-colored medal with a three dimensional image of the Verrazano Bridge, around his neck.

Just after the volunteer presented him with the medal, Adamu heard the coach call out to him.

With tears in his eyes, he walked over to his mentor. As they hugged over a barrier, Adamu sobbed.

In a tone that was more consoling than celebratory, Coach Bellinger told Adamu, "You did great, kid, you really did great. I am proud of you. That was a tremendous effort."

Coach Bellinger had no idea what Adamu's time or place was, but he knew that Adamu had put in a great effort and had just completed a chapter in his life that started well before the 26.2 miles he just ran.

The coach knew that Adamu had faced his pain in a way that he had previously avoided. Coach Bellinger was right—embracing the pain and running with a purpose helped push Adamu to reach his full potential and would ultimately help him move forward in life.

Adamu and Coach Bellinger were interrupted by Jason Schmidt and two other marathon officials.

"Excuse me. Great job, great job. I'm Jason Schmidt with the New York City Marathon. Could you come with us?" he said to Adamu as he pointed over to the tent.

After Adamu told Jason that Mr. Bellinger was his coach, Jason moved the barrier, handed him a pass to wear, and ushered them both into the tent.

"What's going on?" Coach Bellinger asked.

With a facial expression that was partly confused and partly excited, Jason pointed at Adamu and told them, "The computer says that he just ran the fastest time of the day. He even beat the time of the top male finisher. It looks like he just won the marathon."

Still trying to catch his breath, Adamu said, "Hey, Coach."

"What?"

"If I can make it here, I can make it anywhere."

"That's right, kid. You're damn right. And you just made it. Big time."

Mile 24

Huddling around the computer, three senior marathon officials listened closely to Jason Schmidt as he told them the unbelievable news that there was a new winner. As he showed them Adamu's times at various points throughout the race, the number of race officials to join the inquisition, and the volume of their discussions, increased dramatically by the minute.

Doubting officials in the tent mentioned that once a runner cheated to "win" the Boston Marathon by actually running only the last half mile or so of the race. A further investigation revealed that the same person also cheated in the New York City Marathon months earlier when she allegedly took the subway to the finish line.

Those scandals led most races to implement a number of safeguards against cheating, such the use of time chip electronic monitoring systems and video surveillance.

As Allison Millman was talking to the mayor about the particulars of the award ceremony, a marathon official whispered into her ear about the developments involving Adamu.

The expression of shock on her face caused the mayor to inquire if something was wrong. Quickly excusing herself from the conversation, she told the mayor, "They are telling me they think we may have a different winner in the men's race," and then she darted towards the large group of officials in the corner of the tent, which suddenly looked like the floor of the New York Stock Exchange on a busy day of trading.

Onika Dura, who overheard the comment to the mayor, jumped up out of his seat and quickly followed her.

Meanwhile, back on the course William was in the home stretch. Making his way along Central Park South, he was weary, but still running. While disappointed with his time, he was pleased that he did not quit and that he was able to keep jogging until the end. The excited crowds along each side of the street were a good five to seven rows deep.

Up ahead he saw a sign that read "1/2 mile to the finish." While he was not yet at the finish, he knew he would soon make it. He allowed himself to claim victory.

He savored the final cheers of the day and treated the last half mile as a victory lap.

A man in the crowd, smiling and wearing a New York Yankee hat, held up a colorful sign with one hand that said, *"You are all winners."* Attached to the base of the sign on a two-by-four piece of wood was a frying pan with a sticker of a four leaf clover affixed to it. The man furiously swatted the frying pan with a spoon as the runners went by. William gave him a wave, said thank you, and thought *"Only in New York."*

The course continued west to Columbus Circle where it then turned right into Central Park for the approach to the finish line. William looked up at a jumbo screen streaming live footage of the marathon and saw himself. As he ran, he raised his arms and viewed his victorious pose on the screen. He looked liked he belonged. He was about to officially earn the title of marathoner.

Back in Central Park, he and the other runners were rudely welcomed by yet one more incline, but the prospect of having to run up the final hill of the day did not dampen his spirit.

He took it as one last challenge in the long run that he had to meet to be able to earn his achievement. The energetic crowd and the colorful leaves clinging onto the tall trees made it a perfect ending to a long arduous day. He ignored the pain in his knees, managed to smile, and charged up the incline with what little he had left.

With the crowd roaring, he sprinted across the finish line. As he completed a race he never thought he would ever participate in, William was too taxed to feel euphoric. With a finishing time of 4:36:42, he fell short of his goal of four hours, but he did not allow himself to feel anything but satisfaction. He gave it all he had. He did his best.

He realized he made a mistake trying to outrun his pace team, but those were the breaks. He did not meet his goal of completing the race in four hours, but he met his objective of finishing. The experience of training for, participating in, and finishing the biggest marathon in the world had changed the fabric of his being. He had resurrected the athlete within that was dormant for years.

A smiling volunteer approached him and put a marathon medal around his neck. He held the medal and took a good look. It was the first he had earned since college; he had finally come all the way back from his injury.

The emptiness he carried over the years for not being an active part of the Bradford College championship team was filled, just a little, with his marathon finish.

Just past the finish line, an army of photographers were on hand to take pictures of the runners in front of a backdrop with the words "New York City Marathon." William proudly posed for a photo that Christina would later purchase, frame, and display on the mantel above the fireplace in their home.

Wrapped in a tin-foil like blanket handed out by the volunteers, he joined other finishers in a slow and congested walk to retrieve their personal items from one of the many delivery trucks that transported them from Staten Island.

After William got his bag, he dug into it, found his cell phone, and called Nicholas. "I did it kiddo. I finished," he announced after his son answered.

Practically shouting with excitement, Nicholas said, "That's great, Dad, but listen. I got a call from Coach Bellinger just after I saw you in the Bronx. He is in the official's tent at the finish line right now. He said that Adamu won the marathon! That Adamu had the best time of the day!"

"What? Are you kidding me?" William asked loudly.

"He said that even though Adamu got the best time they are not sure if he cheated or not."

"What? Adamu would never cheat. That is ridiculous."

"I am trying to make my way to the officials' tent now. Where are you?"

William, who had just exited Central Park, looked up at the street signs and said, "I am at 72nd Street and Central Park West."

"Okay, I am close by. Stay there I will meet you. Oh, and Dad?"

"What?"

"Congratulations."

Mile 25

Allison Millman, Jason Schmidt, and a host of other race officials continued to look over the computer as they rapidly exchanged their opinions. Standing nearby with a stern look, Onika Dura listened to every word.

Confident of the legitimacy of Adamu's effort—and protective of his "discovery" of the new winner—Jason said more than once, "Look, he had the best time of the day. He is the winner, simple as that."

In response, one of the race officials said, "It is not that simple, Jason. We are not sure if his time is valid. He did not have a camera on him the entire race like the elite runners. He could have taken the subway or something."

Jason quickly responded, "No, it is clear he did not. His chip registered at every checkpoint, and his pace between the checkpoints is consistent. It checks out. He won."

"Jason, we just don't know what happened. He just comes out of nowhere and beats the best runners in the world? He started with the general field for crying out loud. No one has ever heard of him before. "

Another race official added, "What do you want us to do? Put him up there on the winner's podium, and then two days later find out that he is a fraud?"

Standing quietly steps away, with an uninterested look on his face, wearing a thirty-year-old faded heavy cotton uniform of an obscure college track team with the flags of Sudan and the United States, and an Achilles patch haphazardly attached to his tank top with safety pins, Adamu hardly looked like the prototypical picture of the winner of the New York City Marathon.

Standing shoulder to shoulder and face to face with the race officials debating the fate of his victory, wearing sleek high tech athletic apparel bearing the names and logos of his corporate sponsors in bold colors, Onika Dura, who thought just moments earlier that his battles were over for the day, looked even more intense than he did during the race.

William and Nicholas were ushered into the tent by security and quickly met with Adamu and Coach Bellinger, who filled them in on the latest developments.

William hugged Adamu and said, "Incredible job, Adamu. I am so proud of you."

Then, turning into the lawyer he was, he approached the marathon officials to plead Adamu's case in the same confident way he addressed a jury when making a closing statement at a trial.

William introduced himself to the officials and eloquently told them the story of how the honest and good natured Lost Boy from Sudan had endured the loss of his family, friends, and country, survived a long trek to find safe haven, and was now living in Oregon.

He spoke passionately about how he had no doubt that Adamu's time was legitimate. In an attempt to bolster his argument that Adamu be declared the winner, he informed the officials that Adamu had been trained by a highly accomplished coach, and rattled off the impressive times that he ran in the mile, 10K, half-marathon, and in his most recent 23 mile training run.

With deeply focused eyes, Onika Dura moved closer so that he could hear the response of the marathon officials to William's convincing plea.

With a slight smile and a nod of the head acknowledging Adamu and his effort, Allison Millman stepped forward.

Holding a rule book in her hands, she said sincerely, "Listen, I believe in this young man. I do. I really do. But I am sorry to say that we cannot declare him the winner. The rules clearly state that '*the elite races are to be considered separate races apart from the race of the main field.*' The rules go on further to state '*the first three male and female finishers of the elite races are to be declared the first, second, and third place finishers of the New York City Marathon and the medals and trophies that they receive should reflect their place of finish.*' We instituted this rule to make a distinction between the elite runners and the general field. A few years ago we implemented the separate starts for both the elite male and female fields to reinforce this distinction as well as to give the elite runners a clearer path in the streets away from the tens of thousands of runners in the main field so that they could perform in the best conditions. This distinction gives legitimacy to our event. Without it, it would be difficult for us to attract the top runners in the world. What top runner would want to run our marathon if they knew that someone who started a half hour after them had a chance to beat them without them having the opportunity to run side by side against them?"

Ms. Millman paused and again gave Adamu a small smile and a respectful nod.

She then looked back at William and said, "What he did is incredible. It is truly amazing. But I am sorry we cannot declare him the winner."

Reading the rule for himself and hearing Ms. Millman explain the reasonable position of the New York City Marathon just left William shaking his head in agreement.

He wished he could refute the official position with a good reason to change Ms. Millman's mind, but he could not.

He turned to Adamu, who had not uttered a word in the debate, and said "I am sorry, Adamu."

But no apologies were needed.

Adamu accomplished the goal he had formulated in his head the night before—he ran the fastest time in the race. Being declared the "winner" really did not matter to him. He did what he had set out to do.

Ms. Millman and the other officials turned and briskly walked away as another official shouted out that the long delayed podium presentation for the elite men would start in one minute.

Onika Dura and the other top finishers followed the officials out, leaving Adamu, William, Nicholas and Coach Bellinger in the tent alone.

The crowd cheered wildly as Onika Dura took a big step onto the center platform of the winner's podium.

He waved to the crowd as Allison Millman's words reverberated out of the giant speakers nearby, "And for the second year in a row, the winner of the New York City Marathon is Onika Dura of Kenya."

The mayor of New York stepped forward and, as Dura lowered his head, the mayor put the winner's medal around his neck.

Allison Millman then placed a wreath on Dura's head and handed him the winner's trophy. Dura held the trophy, a shiny silver engraved plate, high over his head so the crowd could see it.

Allison Millman then handed Dura a microphone so he could address the crowd.

Dura's initial statement, "Thank you, New York," caused the cheering to intensify. He happily paused to allow the cheering to continue. When it subsided, he continued, "Today was a tough run. The support of the people helped me run my best. I thank you all."

Although it appeared that he was done speaking, he held onto the microphone and continued, "Something happened in today's race that truly amazes me. I learned that a runner who started with the general field ran an incredible race."

Back in the nearby officials' tent, Coach Bellinger, Nicholas, William, and Adamu were watching the award ceremony live on a television. When they heard what Dura said, William, the coach, and Nicholas looked at each other in shock and then at Adamu, whose eyes remained fixed on the television.

After Dura continued by saying, "That runner in the general field even beat my time," an audible confused groan emanated from the crowd.

Quickly responding to the reaction from the crowd, he held up one hand and said, "No, no. This is a good thing. It is a great accomplishment. A truly amazing feat. I believe in this man. He ran with heart and determination. He is a great example of the strength of the people of Southern Sudan. He deserves to be up here on this platform with us. He deserves your applause. So, Adamu, please step up."

William and Nicholas literally lifted Adamu out of his chair and pushed him towards the direction of the winner's platform. When Adamu emerged from the tent, Dura waved at him to step forward. As Adamu got closer to the platform, Onika Dura, the fierce competitor, who would do almost anything to win a race, reached out, pulled him up to the top step, and gave him a big hug.

Nicholas, William, and Coach Bellinger, standing front and center below the winner's platform, joined the crowd, Onika Dura, and the second and third place finishers in cheering Adamu.

It was an incredible, surreal moment. Sensing that Adamu was a little shy and overwhelmed, Dura took hold of Adamu's wrist and pulled Adamu's arm up to the sky. The two fastest runners in the marathon raised their arms in a victory salute as they stood together on the top step of the podium.

"Adamu, introduce yourself to the crowd," Dura said into the microphone, which he handed over to Adamu.

"I am Adamu Jabari. And I am from Southern Sudan." The crowd cheered wildly as they welcomed a new star to the sport—who had just made a spectacular debut on the biggest stage in the world.

Adamu's smile was brighter than the flashes from the multitude of cameras that were taking his picture.

Talking into the microphone he continued, "Thank you. And thank you Onika for sharing this moment with me. I have seen a lot of pain and destruction in Southern Sudan. I dedicate my run to the people of Southern Sudan."

Looking at William, Nicholas, and Coach Bellinger, he added, "I also want to thank my new friends, the Caldwell family, and my coach, Coach Bellinger for his instruction and friendship."

Onika Dura then parted with one of the spoils of his victory by taking the winner's wreath off his head and placing it on Adamu's—causing the cheers of the crowd to intensify.

In the city where everything seemed fast, the taxis darting around town, the subway's shuttling underground, and even the rapid walk of people on the sidewalks, Adamu's speedy achievement stood out.

But more than the speed of his run, it was his story, his heart and determination, and his ability to rise to the top against all odds from a place of pain, despair, and little hope, which made his tale notable in a city with millions of stories.

When the four fastest finishers in the marathon stepped off the podium together, Dick Traum, Nooria Nodrat, and Nano Chilmon from Achilles arrived and congratulated Adamu.

Giving Adamu a big hug, Dick said, "Incredible, Adamu, truly incredible. I told you yesterday that I would see you at the finish line, but I had no idea you would get here so fast!"

"Everyone, can we get a photo together?" an official photographer for the marathon asked loudly.

The group quickly obliged; Onika Dura, Jose Silva, Tafari Botha, Dick Traum, Nooria Nordat, Nano Chilmon, William, Nicholas, and Coach Bellinger turned to the camera and smiled as the photographer snapped away.

In the background, a statue of Fred Lebow looking at a stopwatch was visible—a plaque at its base read *"Few things in life match the thrill of a marathon."*

When the group separated, a horde of reporters descended and swarmed around Adamu. Surrounded by a sea of microphones and cameras, he was suddenly the subject in an impromptu press conference as he was peppered with question after question shouted out from all directions at the same time.

While the always polite Adamu would have been happy to speak with all of them, at that moment, he wanted to have a conversation with just one specific person who was nowhere in sight.

Frantically looking in all directions through the journalists, over the cameras, and past the flashbulbs Adamu could not find him.

Then he spotted him, far up the roadway leading out of Central Park. Suddenly the fastest finisher in the marathon was running again as he dodged around the reporters and the steady stream of other runners milling about after finishing the race.

As he ran up yet another incline for the day, Adamu cupped his hands around the side of his mouth and yelled loudly over the crowd and commotion, "Mr. Traum. Wait. I need to speak with you."

Just before he became part of the packed crowd of people on 72nd Street and Central Park West, Dick Traum, the long established New York City Marathon legend, heard Adamu's call and, with a smile on his face, turned back to have a long talk with the newest New York City Marathon legend.

Mile 26

Back in Oregon days after the marathon, Adamu sat at Nicholas' old desk and carefully wrote out an address on an envelope. After cutting out an article from a newspaper about him "winning" the New York City Marathon, he put it in the envelope and then reached for a piece of paper and began to write:

Dear Kirabo,

Hello, my friend and brother. I am doing fine and I hope this letter finds you well. I realize that it would not have been possible for me to find some peace and happiness in my life without the help of so many people, including you. Even in the worst of times, someone like you, Tahir, and Dr. Zamora helped lead me down the right path. I want you to know how much I appreciate you for enriching my life.

Part of moving forward for me has been the gift of running. I have seen firsthand how running can help the spirit of a person.

One of the great people I met in America is a person named Dick Traum. Like you, when Dick was a young man, he had to get his leg amputated.

Despite losing his leg, Dick kept his spirit strong. He did not let the amputation stop him from running and having a successful life. With a lot of hard work and dedication, Dick became the first person without a leg to run a long distance race called a marathon.

He then started a running club in New York for people with disabilities called the Achilles Track Club where he helps others train so they can participate in running events.

Achilles has organized chapters all over the world. They have even created a chapter called Achilles Kids for children.

Dick has been to many countries and continents, including Africa, to spread the message of Achilles and to help set up chapters. Achilles has also provided many people around the world with free prosthetics.

I have corresponded with Dr. Zamora at the refugee camp and I am happy to say that I will be joining Dick Traum and a group of ambassadors from the United Nations on a trip to the refugee camp in Kenya in December.

You are going to be fitted for a prosthetic leg. Kirabo, you will be able to run and play again! You will be able to run up Lafon Hill or run a marathon one day if you want.

As the article from a newspaper that I have included with this letter says, I just ran the New York City Marathon and had the fastest time out of over 38,000 people.

I was not considered to be the winner of the race because of a rule, but winning does not matter to me. What matters in life is having friends and loved ones – like you – who support, encourage, and stand with you in the most painful of times.

You were right when you told me the opportunity to come to America was a gift. I am thankful you were there to encourage me to accept that gift. I would not have accepted it without you. I have learned it is vital to accept all the gifts life has to offer and to try to create opportunities for others.

I have also learned that, in spite of the physical pain, heartache, or loss we may encounter in life, we must face it head on, move forward, and make the most out of the opportunities we still have.

We are all vulnerable, but I realize, and have seen firsthand, how perseverance in times of weakness can lead to strength and accomplishment.

I know that you have the strength to move on, for it was you that provided me with strength.

I am looking forward to seeing you. I can't wait to run with you.

Your brother,
Adamu

Although his legs were still sore days after the marathon, William practically skipped into work with a hop in his step.

While his workload was hectic because everything got backed up while he was in New York, William sat down at his desk with a renewed spirit. He realized how right Christina was when she said that, for him to get out of his funk, he had to think outside of the box and do things that were not necessarily in his comfort zone.

A framed copy of the picture of him with Coach Bellinger, Adamu, Nicholas, the top male finishers, and members of the Achilles team sat on his desk. While on a conference call, he looked at the photograph and, for a few seconds, happily lost track of what was being said on the phone. What was truly important in life was captured in the photo.

The picture signified so many things to William: family, friendship, loyalty, love, sacrifice, and a healthy lifestyle. He still recognized that work was important, but he would put it in its proper place. He would not let it control his life. Forging relationships, taking care of himself, and spending time with loved ones was the priority.

For William, the greater satisfaction and sense of accomplishment about finishing the marathon came days after he crossed the finish line. He appreciated how the whole experience, the arduous training, as well as the marathon itself, showed him he could push further than he thought possible.

When he first reviewed the marathon training program Coach Bellinger constructed, he thought it was impossible. But with hard work and a mental spirit that, like his body, got stronger, he was able to complete the training. The experience transferred over to other aspects of his life as well as he felt he could more easily push forward in the face of frustration.

He realized, as it was inevitable that a runner would face a struggle in a marathon, it was certain there would be struggles in life. The only choice was to push forward with positive thoughts.

The marathon also helped him rediscover his love of running. He realized he should not have allowed his injury in college to prevent him from running.

He let his injury become an excuse, a reason to stay on the couch. He was still an athlete who loved to run and compete. In fact, even though he thought more than once during the later miles of the marathon when he was struggling that he would never run another one, he already had the itch to try again. He regretted his decision to try to outrun his pace team and believed that he might have met his goal time if he had just run a smarter race.

After the conference call finished, William searched on his computer for when the next marathon in the area was scheduled. Then he started a search for a surprise gift for his wife—a trip to Paris.

After he finished emptying the last box from the move years earlier, Coach Bellinger headed to the mantel in the living room.

He carefully organized the framed pictures of his wife and gave some of the old championship trophies from his college days as a runner and as a coach an additional shine.

He positioned the plaque and the photos his old team gave him at the surprise party on the mantel next to a framed picture of him and Adamu standing beside the bicycle Adamu had bought for him.

Then he reached down for one more framed picture and placed it in the last empty space on the mantel. With admiration and amazement he looked at the picture of him, Adamu, William, Nicholas, the top male finishers, and members of the Achilles team taken after the marathon.

Stepping back a few feet to take it all in, he thought about how special it was to have been married to such a wonderful wife and to have been a part of so many championships and then, after he was retired, to train a runner who had the fastest time at the New York City Marathon.

It had truly been a whirlwind couple of days. Adamu's achievement was huge news. It made the cover of the New York newspapers and many magazines, and he joined Adamu for interviews on many television and radio shows.

He was proud of the part he played in the historic event and was touched by Adamu's recognition of his contribution.

He shook his head side to side in proud disbelief at what he saw displayed before him on the mantel. So many stories, so many lives, so much love.

He felt a sense of satisfaction and achievement and, in some way, a rebirth. His life had meaning again. While he would continue to endure the disappointment of not having children, he realized that all of the kids he coached were, in a way, his children. Training William and Adamu helped remind him that it was important to stay active so he could remain connected with people. He recognized he still had something to offer, and that, through coaching, he could find fulfillment and purpose.

He eagerly looked forward to joining the coaching staff at the local Achilles chapter, which was just a short ride away on his new bike.

The three-man team of Adamu, Coach Bellinger, and William had been on a marathon journey together.

Although they were each reluctant to take the first steps in their journey, they were moved in the right direction by people who loved and cared for them.

Along the way, reluctance gave way to eagerness. Fear was overcome by courage. Despair was replaced by inspiration and hope. Loneliness lost out to friendship.

After putting the letter to Kirabo in the envelope and sealing it, Adamu opened the desk drawer and pulled out the photo album that Christina gave him.

He opened it and peeled back the clear sheet on one of the empty pages. He then picked up a copy of the photo of him with Coach Bellinger, William, Nicholas, the top male finishers, and members of the Achilles team taken after the marathon, and carefully centered it on the page.

Then he secured it on the page by covering it with the clear sheet.

Looking at the photo he started to think about the moment he and his friends stood on top of Lafon Hill. He wished he had a photo of that moment to put in the photo album, but his heart was the only place where that image could be found.

He closely studied his face in the picture.

He recalled experiencing virtually the same happiness at the time he was on top of Lafon Hill with his friends as he did in New York when the photo was taken. And the happiness he experienced at each moment was not because he finished each race first or with the best time—it was because he was in the presence of friends and people that he loved.

He was amazed and thankful that he was able to reach that same level of happiness again after all he had lost.

With tears falling from his eyes, and a smile on his face, he closed the photo album.

At one time he thought it would be impossible to fill up all the pages in the album with pictures because he believed that all the meaningful moments in his life were in the past. He thought he would never be able to experience moments in the future that would be important enough to capture in a photo.

Now he fully expected that he would add more photos to the many empty pages still left in the album.

In fact, he was going to see to it that the entire photo album would be filled.

Adamu was ready to create more memories in the story that was his life.

A few months later, Adamu added the next entry to his photo album. It was a picture of him with Kirabo, Tahir, Dr. Zamora, and Dick Traum, standing under a clear blue Kenyan sky after they all completed a run together.

Kirabo, the newest member of the Achilles team, was smiling broadly.

Afterword

While *Marathon Journey, An Achilles Story* is fictional, Achilles International and its athletes, including myself, are real.

In May of 1965, at 24, I lost my right leg above the knee after being hit by a car at a gas station on the New Jersey Turnpike. Although earning a BS, MBA, and Ph.D., and having a successful career, ten years after the accident I was out of shape.

After a peer my age had a heart attack, an associate suggested my joining the West Side YMCA. The instructor at the YMCA said everybody—even the guy with one leg—had to run for ten minutes. Having never considered it, I began running by taking a hop and a step, as if one were rushing across a street with a cast on his leg.

Eventually, ten minutes was easy and a mile became comfortable. In May of 1976, I completed my first race, a five-miler in Central Park. On October 24, 1976, I completed the New York City Marathon, becoming the first amputee to run such a distance—it was one of the most exciting days of my life. Completing the Marathon was a life-changing experience which provided me with a powerful sense of achievement and boosted my self-esteem.

Inspired by my story, a young man in Canada, Terry Fox, who had his right leg amputated as a result of cancer, attempted to run across Canada in 1980 to raise money for cancer research. Terry's courageous "Marathon of Hope" made him a national hero in Canada and an inspiration around the world.

In turn, Terry Fox inspired me to create an eight week running program for people with disabilities. In 1983, seeking to provide that same opportunity for others, Achilles was founded.

Today, Achilles International has chapters and members in over 70 locations within the United States and abroad. Every day, in parks, gyms, and tracks all over the world, Achilles provides athletes with disabilities with a community of support where disabled runners and able-bodied volunteers come together to train and compete. Within this community, runners gain a measurable physical strength and build confidence through their sense of accomplishment, which often transfers to other parts of their lives.

Over the years, Achilles has also developed specialized programs for children and war veterans. *Achilles Kids* provides training, racing opportunities, and an in-school program for children with disabilities. Our *Freedom Team of Wounded Veterans* brings running programs and marathon opportunities to disabled veterans.

While our programs focus on athletics, the truth is, sports are simply the tool for accomplishing our main objective: to bring hope, inspiration, and the joys of achievement to people with disabilities.

Achievement is addictive and contagious. Each success increases the expectations of what is possible in the future. Self-esteem improves with each triumph, as does the level of aspiration.

While we all have different types of vulnerability, I agree with one of the messages in *Marathon Journey, An Achilles Story* that perseverance in times of weakness can lead to strength.

Moreover, as illustrated in the story, when Adamu, William, and Coach Bellinger find inspiration, hope, and fulfillment as they become a team, I strongly believe that the opportunity for achievement increases by being part of a group.

Join our team as a volunteer, member, or supporter *(achillesinternational.org)*.

Go Achilles!

Dick Traum
New York City, December 2012

The author would like to thank and acknowledge:

A very special thanks to Dick Traum. Not only was Dick Traum a source of inspiration for the story, he was instrumental in helping it become a finished product. I greatly appreciate the time, advice, and encouragement he gave me throughout the process of writing the story. The story would not have been published without Dick Traum. Include me on the long—and ever growing—list of people that Dick Traum helped to reach their goal.

Dick Traum's positive influence, accomplishments, and contributions to the sport of running cannot be overstated. He is a true marathon legend.

To learn more about Dick Traum and Achilles—and to support the team, visit: *achillesinternational.org* and read *"Go Achilles!"* by Dick Traum and Mary Bryant.

Thank you to Achilles athletes Nooria Nodrat, Nano Chilmon, and Zoe Koplowitz for their inspirational example and for allowing me to use them as real life "characters" in the story. They are more than deserving of all the cheers and accolades they receive on and off of the course.

Nooria Nodrat is the President of the Afghanistan Blind Women and Children Foundation (*theabwcfoundation.org*) where she is seeking to enhance the lives of Afghani blind women and children through education and health services.

Zoe Koplowitz is the author of *"The Winning Spirit"*.

Aidan Walsh, thank you for your time and thoughts.

Thank you to: the volunteers, spectators, participants, organizers, and sponsors of the New York City Marathon, the Philadelphia Marathon, and the Long Beach Island 18 Mile Run (Long Beach Island, NJ). Achilles International, The Lost Boys of Sudan, Runner's World Magazine, The New York Road Runner's Club, Professor Brooks Landon.

Mom and Dad, thank you for your guidance, support, and example.

Regina, thank you for everything—including introducing us to the marathon (over my initial cowardly objections). I look forward to completing the miles of life ahead with you.

Made in the USA
Charleston, SC
04 December 2013